# THIS
# STRANGER
# MY SON

ELIZABETH BAKER

# THIS
# STRANGER
# MY SON

*Illustrated by*
*Beth and Joe Krush*

Houghton Mifflin Company Boston 1971

OTHER BOOKS BY

ELIZABETH BAKER

Fire in the Wind
Stronger Than Hate
Tammy Camps in the Rocky Mountains
Tammy Camps Out
Tammy Climbs Pyramid Mountain
Tammy Goes Canoeing
Treasures of Rattlesnake Hill

For S.H.B.

# THIS
# STRANGER
# MY SON

# Chapter One

MARC PUSHED his long, stringy hair away from his eyes and leaned forward to peer through the rain-covered windshield of the small red Volkswagen. "Watch out, Steve," he warned the driver. "There's a great big puddle under the overpass."

Steve stepped on the brake and the small car slowed with a jerk just before the front wheels plowed into several inches of water collected in a dip in the road.

"All I can say is, I'm glad this isn't snow," Steve muttered as the little car crawled along cautiously, water flying in wings away from the wheels.

"Hey, there's a hitchhiker on the other side of the puddle. It's a girl. Shouldn't we pick her up? She looks pretty unhappy."

Steve glanced to his right and caught a glimpse of a

girl with long, kinky red hair leaning against the wall of the bridge pier, her thumb held out halfheartedly. "I can't stop now. I might stall."

"We can't just go by and leave her."

Steve sighed and pulled the little car over to the shoulder just beyond the overpass. Marc flung open his door and leaned out.

"Want a ride?"

The girl stared at him for a moment, then picked up the knobby, khaki-colored pack at her feet and trotted to the car. Marc pulled the back of his seat forward and grabbed the pack as the girl squeezed past him into the back seat.

Steve downshifted. The little car sputtered and choked as it crawled up the hill. The girl took off her felt hat with its big drooping brim, pushed back her long wet hair, and brushed at the sleeves of her stained, shapeless khaki jacket. Marc dropped her pack over the back of his seat and smiled at her.

"Kind of a wet day to be on the road."

She nodded.

"Where you heading for?"

"I don't know. Any place will do."

"We're only going to Warton."

"Never heard of it."

"It's only about five miles from here."

"That's okay."

"What'll you do then?"

She shrugged and stuck out her thumb.

"It'll be dark pretty soon. And the rain isn't going to let up tonight."

"Stop pestering me, will you? I can take care of myself."

"Sorry," Marc said.

"That's okay." The girl rubbed the steam off the small window beside her and looked out at the wet highway.

"You been on the road long?" Marc asked after a silence.

"I left town after lunch."

"You should be going south, not west, this time of year."

"Maybe. But the first ride I got was going this way, so I took it. I was in kind of a rush to leave."

They drew up at a red light at a large intersection. Steve looked over his shoulder at the girl. "Here's where we turn off for Warton. Shall we let you out?"

She looked out again. "I suppose this is as good a place as any to get a long ride."

Steve drove across the intersection and pulled over to the side of the road. The girl hoisted her pack up from the floor.

"Steve, we can't just leave her in the rain and drive away," Marc protested. "Suppose nobody picks her up. She'll be here all night."

"What do you want to do?"

"We could take her to Ben Barker's cabin."

"I suppose we could do that." Steve turned to the girl again. "You a runaway?"

"How'd you guess?" she said sarcastically.

Steve turned to Marc. "You can get into trouble for harboring runaways."

"You don't need to worry. My parents aren't looking for me."

"How long have you been away from home?" Marc asked.

"Three months and three weeks next Saturday. I left early in August."

"Where you from?"

"Chicago."

"You on your way home?" Steve asked.

She shook her head so hard drops of water flew off the ends of her mane of hair. "I'm never going home."

"Do you want to stay in this cabin we know about overnight, or at least until the rain stops?"

"You won't tell anyone I'm there?"

"No, we won't," Marc promised. "You can trust us."

"It's a good cabin," Steve said. "The roof doesn't leak and the windows aren't broken and there's lots of dry firewood."

"If you decided you wanted to stay for a while," Marc added, "we could come back later tonight and bring you some food and a sleeping bag. There's a good stove in the cabin, too."

"That might be kind of fun. I haven't slept out since I went to summer camp up in Canada when I was a kid."

Steve looked at the girl in his rear vision mirror. "You don't look so old now."

"You don't look so old yourself," the girl snapped.

"He's going to college next year," Marc said.

"Are you going to college, too?"

Marc shook his head. "Not if I can help it."

Steve turned off the paved road onto a dirt road with a high, gravelly crown. The girl looked out at the wet leafless woods on either side. "It's pretty lonely in here. How far is this cabin?"

Steve stopped the car. "Not much farther, but we'd better walk the rest of the way. The road is getting pretty muddy."

With Marc in the lead carrying the girl's pack, they slogged single file through the woods. The rain drummed steadily on their heads and shoulders. The wet pine needles and oak leaves under their feet squished spongily. The girl shivered and pulled up the collar of her jacket.

"Are you sure there's a cabin in this woods?"

"On top of that rise." Steve pointed. "The shingles are gray. That's why it's so hard to see it through the trees."

Marc pushed open the cabin door and stood aside to let the girl go in ahead of him. She stood in the middle of the rough plank floor and looked around the small bare room. The dimming gray light shone in faintly through the small dusty windows. She shivered. "It's cold in here."

"We'll get a fire going in a minute." Steve jerked open the door to the lean-to woodshed.

Marc pointed to the bed-sized raised shelf in one of the corners. "That's really quite comfortable with an air mattress and a sleeping bag."

"I'm used to hard beds." The girl unzipped her jacket. "I've been sleeping on the floor for weeks."

Steve came back with an armload of kindling and logs and dropped them on the floor. As he laid a fire in the stove the girl wandered around restlessly.

"Are there any other houses near here?"

"Not for miles," Marc said. "Don't worry. No one will find you."

"I haven't been by myself in ages. It'll seem funny not to have someone stepping on me when I'm trying to sleep or cooking up spaghetti in the middle of the night or suddenly deciding to have a party or paint a picture or play the guitar at some crazy time."

"Sounds like an interesting life," Marc said wistfully.

"It was never boring."

Steve struck a match and held it to the newspaper he had crumpled up and stuffed into the stove. In a moment, the kindling caught fire and heat began to pour out into the room. The girl crept up to the stove on her hands and knees and knelt with her back to the open door.

"Of course we didn't always have regular meals."

Marc smiled. "That probably would be good for me. My father's always telling me I'm too fat."

"I hate people that make personal remarks."

"What can you do if it's your parents?"

"Tell them to stop."

"My dad isn't the kind you give orders to. He likes too much to give orders himself."

The girl tipped her head and spread out one side of her hair in front of the fire. "I know. It's a pain."

Marc sighed. "Everything I do is wrong."

"What kind of things do you do?" The girl flipped her hair behind her shoulders and shook it while she looked up at him.

"Not much really. If I was making the drug scene or messing around with girls or stealing cars or something like that I'd figure he had a right to complain, but to get mad because I cut classes to go into town to a peace demonstration isn't fair. Two times I cut classes, and you should have heard the noise. My job at the moment, he says, is to get an education and not bother about politics."

The girl combed her fingers through her hair and shook it again. "What's your mother like?"

Marc looked over at Steve. "What would you say my mom was like?"

"Nervous." Steve picked up a stick of kindling and tossed it into the stove. "Hops around like a scared bird."

"That's what she is. Scared. Never relaxes for a minute for fear something will go wrong and Dad will get mad. My sister Sharon can get away with anything, but not me."

"Does she drink?"

"She doesn't have to. My dad drinks enough for them both."

The girl stood up, pulled off her steaming jacket, and tossed it onto the pile of wood beside the stove. "What about you? What are your folks like?" She jerked her head at Steve, who was perched on the edge of one of the sleeping shelves.

Steve grinned. "I'm not complaining."

"You shouldn't," Marc said. "There's nothing wrong with your parents. You don't know how lucky you are not to have your mother always getting after you about something — your clothes or your homework or going to some party at the country club, or your dad picking a fight with you about your hair or your ideas or your future."

"That's because I'm such a square."

"The dullest people I know are the ones who never have any trouble with their parents," the girl said.

"That's me. Dull as they come." Steve brushed some bark off his sleeve, looked at his wrist watch, and stood up. "We've got to go, Marc. It's almost six o'clock."

"Where do you live?"

"Down the river. It's not far from here by canoe. That's the way we come in the summer. By road it's about three miles."

"River?"

"Yes, there's a river in front of the cabin. Didn't you notice? There's a path through the woods to the place where we land our boats. In the morning, you can take a walk down there."

"No, thanks. I might get lost. Are you sure you have to go?"

Marc nodded. "My father just got a big promotion at work and Mom's having a party to celebrate. She'd have a fit if we weren't there."

"Why does he have to go?" The girl looked at Steve.

"He's my cousin. His father and mine are brothers."

The girl followed them to the door. "Mind telling me your names?"

"I'm Marc and he's Steve. Marc and Steve Ainsworth. What's yours?"

The girl's eyes narrowed suspiciously. "Why do you want to know?"

"We have to call you something. Make up something if you don't want to tell us your real name."

"I used to wish my name was Ann."

"Okay, we'll call you Ann."

"I wouldn't know who you were talking to. You'd better just call me Tally like everyone else does. It's short for Natalie."

"Okay, Tally, as soon as we can get away from this party we'll bring you up some food and a sleeping bag," Steve promised.

"I hope you don't get too hungry," Marc added.

"I'm used to not eating."

"Bread kind of hard to come by when you're a runaway?" Steve asked.

"Sure is. People are pretty stingy."

"Were you panhandling?"

"Anything wrong with that?"

"Doesn't have much of a future."

"Who cares about the future? Live for today, man. At the rate the world is going there won't be any future."

"I wish more people understood that," Marc said eagerly. "Everybody just goes along in their blind, self-satisfied way doing nothing while the world is breaking up around us."

Steve tugged on the sleeve of his cousin's faded, rain-spotted denim jacket. "It's going to break up sooner than you think if we're late for dinner."

"Do you really want to go to this party?" Tally asked.

"Not especially," Steve said. "I've got a history paper I should be working on."

"How about you?" Tally stared at Marc.

"I don't want to go, but how can I get out of it? After all, it is my dad."

"So what? If you don't want to do a thing, don't do it."

Steve looked at her with his eyes narrowed. "You really believe that?"

"Sure I do. I can't stand hypocrisy."

"Me neither," Marc said fiercely.

"Well, stay if you want to." Steve stepped off the doorstep onto the muddy path. "I'm on my way."

"Wait a minute. I'm coming." Marc turned around on the big doorstone. "Bye, Tally. I hope you stick around for a while. This town needs some-one like you."

"You'd better watch that girl," Steve said as they slogged back to the car. "If she sticks around long there'll be trouble."

"Because she believes in being totally honest? The trouble with you, Steve, is you're too anxious to please people."

Steve laughed. "Maybe so. But a little oil certainly

11

makes life's machinery run more smoothly."

"How are things going to get changed if everyone just goes along oiling the machinery?" Marc climbed in the car and slammed the door.

"You'll be sure and bring along a sleeping bag and some cans of food tonight?" he said as they drew up in front of his house. "If I try to do anything, my mother or Sharon will ask me a million questions."

Steve nodded. "I'm not sure how we'll get away."

"We'll think of something when the time comes. See you in a while." Marc waved and trudged across the wet lawn to the house.

# Chapter Two

MARC SAT at the dinner table with his head down, concentrating on his food. He had just put the last spoonful of chocolate mousse into his mouth when his Uncle Julius, sitting across the table from him, tapped on the rim of his long-stemmed goblet with his spoon and stood up.

"I'd like to propose a toast."

The conversation died and everyone stood up, holding his goblet of amber-colored cider. "To Marcus Ainsworth," Julius said solemnly. "May this promotion not be his last."

The man at the far end of the table smiled at Julius. "Why so formal, Jules? No one's called me Marcus since Grandma died."

"I couldn't call you Budge on such a formal occasion, could I?"

"Is it a formal occasion? Marc doesn't seem to think so." Budge frowned at his son, then looked down the table at his wife. "Jean, can't you make this boy wear anything except those ragged black jerseys and old blue jeans?"

Jean's thin face flushed and she set her goblet down quickly. "Never mind, never mind," Budge said quickly. "Let's not let anything spoil the occasion. Thank you, Jules, for your kind wishes. If you'd stayed with United Products, I'm sure we'd be having the party in your honor. And thank you, Jeannie, for the lovely surprise. And thank you all for coming." He sat down, leaned back in his armchair, and smoothed the hair at his temple lightly with the fingers of his right hand.

"Was the party really a surprise, Budge?" Jean leaned sideways in her chair so she could see her husband around the centerpiece of yellow and white flowers.

"You know, Velma," she said to her sister-in-law, "he came out into the kitchen last night when I was making the chocolate mousse. I was so afraid he'd notice what I was doing and ask what it was for, since he knows that chocolate mousse is my favorite party dessert. But he never said a word. All he wanted was to ask me to type up a report on the year's golf season at the country club for the next board of governor's meeting. If he'd asked me about the mousse, I don't know what I'd have said. I'm no good at lying. One look at my face and he'd have known I wasn't making chocolate mousse for the bridge club."

Velma laughed. "I don't think Julius would know if I was making chocolate mousse or boiling an egg. He's been so preoccupied lately with business that I'm not sure he even knows I'm around, let alone what I'm doing."

"How is business?" Budge turned toward his brother. "I still don't understand why you left U.P. to go off and start your own company."

"Maybe he got tired of making things that kill people," Marc muttered.

Jean jumped up hastily. "Let's not spoil the evening by talking business. You all go into the living room and Sharon and I'll bring the coffee in there. It's all ready and will only take a minute to put on the tray. Go on, Velma, you take everybody in there and get them comfortable. Come on, Sharon."

When she came into the living room a few minutes later carrying the large silver tray, Budge and Julius were lounging side by side on the sofa placed at a right angle to the fireplace. Steve and Marc were in the corner behind them looking through a stack of records. Sharon put down the dish of salted nuts she was carrying and hurried to look over Steve's shoulder at the record he was holding.

Jean placed the tray on the table and sat down. "Now, Julius, you like one sugar and a little cream, don't you?"

"That coffee looks pretty strong. Make it two sugars and lots of cream."

"Budge?"

"I'll have mine black. You ought to watch it, Jules. Jean just loaded about a hundred and thirty-six calories into that cup for you."

"Is that right?" Julius gazed thoughtfully at the pale brown liquid he was slowly stirring. "How do you know?"

Budge pulled a small booklet out of the breast pocket of his suit coat. "I have a calorie chart. You'd be surprised how many calories you can cut out with a little thought. Cut out rolls and butter at lunch and right there is about a hundred and fifty. And by giving up bacon for breakfast and having my egg boiled instead of fried, I cut out a hundred and forty. You ought to try it." He laid the booklet on his brother's knee. "I'll give you this. I have another one."

"Why should I start counting calories? It'll take all the pleasure out of eating."

Budge slapped his brother's stomach with the back of his hand. "You're not getting any thinner, old man. Besides, it doesn't look well for a corporate executive to be fat. People won't have any confidence in you. They'll think you're lazy, slow on your feet. You've got to look trim, vigorous, youthful."

Julius looked sideways at Budge. "I can't believe you were made head of the sales division of United Products just for your good looks."

In the corner by the record player Sharon exclaimed sharply, "No, Marc, not that one. Steve doesn't want it and I'm sick of it. Play this one."

16

Budge turned and glared at them. "What's the matter?"

"We can't decide what records to put on, Daddy." Sharon smiled coaxingly and held up two record covers. "Which one do you want?"

"Neither." Budge waved his hand disgustedly. "I can't stand the music you kids listen to. Either it's just a lot of noise or it's some singer whining and crying about how hard life is."

"Turn on the FM," Velma suggested. "Symphony should be on."

"Whatever you play, keep it low." Budge turned back to Julius. "So you were able to get the capital you needed to expand into that new product line?"

"I did. And now all I need is you to run my expanded sales department." Julius set his empty cup down on the table and clapped his brother on the shoulder. "How about it? Vice president in charge of sales? A nice chunk of Envirotronics stock? And about a hundredth the pressure you're living under now trying to keep United Products' sales chart upward bound."

Budge smiled and shook his head. "No go, brother. Compared to United Products, Envirotronics doesn't count for beans in the industrial world. I'll stay where I am and who knows, someday I might be president."

"We make a good product, one that's going to make the world a better place to live in."

"What's wrong with the products we make?"

"If this country ever decides to cut its defense budget, those sales charts of yours could suffer."

18

"War is a fact of life."

"Is the rumor true I heard that U.P. might be going to buy Brown Chemical?"

"It's not a rumor. It's a fact. The acquisition will be announced next week. What's wrong with Brown Chemical? It's a very sound company and will give us good diversification."

"Don't they make nerve gas and other stuff for the army?"

Budge snapped his fingers. "That's only a small part of their production. Besides, someone has to make those things. What would happen to this country if no one manufactured weapons for her defense?"

Julius gazed at Budge for a moment, his face sober. "Well, if you change your mind, let me know."

"Hey, fella." Budge balled his fist and pushed his brother lightly on the chin. "Cheer up. We're celebrating my promotion, not attending my funeral. You need a drink. What'll you have?"

Julius held up his hands and shook his head.

"Come on, come on." Budge jumped up and went over to the bar table between the two front windows. "One little nightcap isn't going to hurt a thing. What'll you have?"

"Nothing. And if you'll take your big brother's advice you won't have any more tonight, either."

Budge turned around, a glass full of ice cubes in his hand. "Now look here, Julius. You may be my big brother but that doesn't give you any right to tell me what to do. I make more money than you do and before long I'll make even more — if what I suspect is in the cards comes true and I become a vice president and director of U.P. So if I want a drink after dinner I guess I'm big enough to know whether I can handle it or not."

Budge turned around again and poured his drink while the other three near the fireplace looked at each other in embarrassment and then glanced away. "What are you children doing?" Jean called brightly toward the three in the corner. "Why don't you put on a nice record that all of us would enjoy? How about the music from *My Fair Lady?*"

"Steve and Marc are saying they want to go for a ride in Uncle Julius's new sports car," Sharon pouted.

"Go for a ride, now, in all this rain?" Jean jumped up and pulled back the heavy brocade drapery over one of the front windows. "Why, it's pouring down in buckets. Why do you want to go for a ride?"

"It's nice riding in the rain," Marc said.

Jean came around the couch and drew Marc into the corner beside the record player. "I can't tell Steve what to do," she said in a low angry voice, "but you cannot walk out on your father's party. It was bad enough your coming in that awful old black jersey and those patched, ragged blue jeans, but to want to leave before the party's over is terrible and I won't let you. Do you hear?"

"Okay, Mom." Marc shrugged resignedly and threw himself into an armchair.

"It was just a wild idea of mine, Aunt Jean." Steve smiled apologetically. "Tell you what, Sharon. I just remembered I bought a neat new record this

20

afternoon at the Coop when Marc and I went into Harvard Square. You'll love it. I'll go home and get it. That way I'll get to drive Dad's car a little all by myself and still won't miss the rest of the party. Okay, Dad?"

"Sure, Steve. Want my keys?"

"No, thanks, I have mine." As Steve went out he looked back over his shoulder at Marc. Marc lifted his hand just a little from the arm of the chair and let it drop.

Sharon looked at him suspiciously but didn't say anything.

"How about a game of cards, everyone?" Jean jumped up and pulled open the shallow drawer in a small mahogany table. "Marc, Sharon, how about all of us playing Hearts?"

"We really must be going," Velma said.

"You can't go until Steve comes back with your car." Jean took a pack of cards out of a box and shuffled it. "Marc, dear, get the card table out of the hall closet. And Sharon, the card-table cover is in the bottom drawer of the chest in the hall."

When everyone was gathered around the card table Jean jumped up again. "We'll need something to keep score on. Somebody go ahead and deal while I get a piece of paper and a pencil from the kitchen. And remember to leave two cards in the kitty."

She hurried back into the room and sat down quickly. "Here, dear, you keep score. You're so good at figures." She put the paper and pencil in front of Budge and scooped up the pile of cards at her place.

"Now let's see. What three cards can I pass on, Julius, that will really make trouble for you?"

"Are you playing that the jack of diamonds is worth ten points?" Velma asked.

"That's sissy." Marc frowned at his cards, picked out three, and passed them to his sister.

"I don't think it's sissy at all," Sharon said. "I think we should count the jack of diamonds."

"Okay, we'll count the jack of diamonds." Budge picked up the cards that Velma had passed to him and groaned.

She grinned at him. "What's the matter? Did you just clear your hand of that suit?"

"How'd you guess? Who leads?"

"I do." Marc threw out the two of clubs. When the hand was finished, Jean leaned back in her chair and sighed happily as Julius gathered up the cards and began to shuffle them.

"Isn't this fun? Doesn't it remind you of the old days, Velma, when we'd all play Hearts together on rainy days on the screened porch at Grandma Ainsworth's cottage at the lake? The boys seemed to have so much more time then to spend with their families. Why, Budge would sooner die now than take a Friday and Monday off and spend a long weekend at the lake. We haven't been up there in years. I'm afraid we've let you do all the work of keeping it up and renting it."

"We were up over Labor Day." Velma fanned out her cards and studied them. "It was in pretty good shape. The porch foundations need replacing. Mr. Stourby is going to care of it in the spring."

"Is he still around?" Budge looked up from his cards. "He must be a hundred and ten by now. He was ancient when we were kids."

Julius laughed. "He probably was all of thirty when we were kids. Yes, he's still around and going strong. Say, I forgot to tell you. The old Danby farmhouse on the hill above the lake and about fifty acres of land have been bought by a bunch of hippies and they've got a commune going."

"No kidding? Complete with dope and vegetarian food and everybody making love to everybody else and nobody knowing whose children are whose?"

"That's not the way real communes are at all." Marc glared defiantly at his father.

"I beg your pardon," Budge said sarcastically. "I should have remembered that I've been told communes are really all love and peace, mind expansion, plain living, high thinking, and very good influences on the communities in which they are located."

Julius closed up his hand and tapped the table with the cards. "As a matter of fact, Mr. Stourby seemed quite fond of the people in this commune. They've set up a shop which sells organic foods, candles, hand-woven fabrics, and pottery, which seems to draw quite a steady stream of customers who spill a little cash in the town on their way out to the farm. Also, they've been running a program for the children in the town, which was a great success, and I guess they're going to continue it this winter. You know yourself there isn't much for a kid to do in Centre Danby."

Budge held up his hand and grinned. "Stop. If you're not careful we'll have Marc running away to join them. He considers our suburban life pretty superficial and materialistic."

Marc's chubby cheeks turned an angry red. Jean hastily patted his hand and shook her head warningly. "I don't see what's taking Steve so long to get that record," Sharon complained.

Velma looked at her watch. "Oh, Julius, it is late. Maybe we'd better walk. It's only half a mile and I could use the exercise after that lovely dinner Jean gave us. I wore my raincoat and boots."

"There he is," Jean said. "I just heard him drive in."

Marc turned and stared out into the hall. Steve stamped in, caught his cousin's eye, raised his right hand, touched the tips of his thumb and third finger together in an O and nodded. Marc nodded in return and turned back to the table.

"Where's the record, Steve?" Sharon asked.

Steve took a record out from under his coat. "I forgot I left it in the Volkswagen and was looking for it all over the house. That's what took me so long."

"We don't have time for you to play it now, dear." Velma pushed back her chair. "It's been a lovely evening, Jean. Budge, congratulations again on the new honor. You certainly deserve it. I don't know a man who works any harder than you do."

As the grownups moved into the hall, Sharon clutched Marc's arm, digging her long fingernails through his jersey into his skin. "You two have a secret."

Marc pressed his lips together and stared straight ahead.

"You can't keep a secret from me," she hissed. "I'll find out what it is. You just wait and see."

# Chapter Three

I saw miss tracey," Marc said as he and Steve hurried toward the high school parking lot the next afternoon after school. "She said she'd adjourn the meeting to her house. I told her we'd be there in three quarters of an hour."

"That won't give us much time to talk to Tally." Steve pulled out his keys and unlocked the red Volkswagen. "She may be getting lonesome by now."

"I didn't see what else I could do. Mobilization for Peace Day is next Wednesday and we haven't made any plans at all for our participation in it. I wish the national committee had sent out their letter sooner."

"Who else besides members of the Foreign Affairs club do you think will be interested in the demonstration?"

"That's the problem. It's so late we won't have time to put anything in the town newspaper about the school demonstration, although there'll be something in this week's issue about the silent vigil around the town flagpole that Reverend Cumberland is leading. And, of course, we missed this month's issue of the school paper."

"You can put up some posters around the school."

"If we find someone to make them." Marc stared gloomily at the ragged toes of his dirty sneakers. "Have you ever noticed how hard it is to get people to work for something they say they believe in?"

Steve nodded. "Did Mr. Johnson say it was all right to hold a demonstration?"

"Miss Tracey is going to ask him when we have our plans made. She says she knows he won't give us a blank check. I don't see why he doesn't trust us."

"I think he does trust you, only he has the taxpayers to consider, too. There are still a lot of people in town who feel peace is the same thing as giving in to the communists."

Marc sighed. "Do you suppose the time will ever come when people will stop sacrificing an obviously good idea like peace to the power of money?"

"Not everyone sees things in such simple terms as you do, Marc."

"All the great reformers have thought in simple terms. They had one idea, and that was what they put first. The minute you begin to lower your sights and make compromises, your cause fails."

"You may be right. Do you want something to

eat? There's a bag of cookies in that bag of groceries for Tally."

Marc knelt on the seat and rummaged in the brown paper bag on the back seat. "You stopped around before school this morning to see her?"

Steve slowed for the turn into the dirt road. "She said the air mattress leaked and the sleeping bag smelled musty."

"She did? I didn't think she cared about things like that."

"She's not as tough as she tries to make you think she is."

Marc took several cookies and put the bag on the seat beside him. "How much do I owe you for my share of this stuff?"

"Do you have any money? I thought you weren't taking your allowance from your dad because you don't like how his company makes its money."

"I take it but I send it all to CARE."

"All of it?"

"What's the point if I don't send it all?"

"But what do you do for money? You have to have some."

"Ever hear of earning it? I do odd jobs on Saturdays for a couple of old ladies in the center of town. Take out the trash, rake leaves, wash windows, whatever they want."

"Does your dad know what you're doing with your allowance?"

"I haven't had a chance to tell him. There never

28

seems to be a good time. Either he's not home or he has something else on his mind or we've just had a big argument about something."

"Hey," Steve exclaimed. "There's Tally coming down the road."

"She has her pack on." As soon as Steve stopped the car Marc opened the door and hopped out. "Where are you going?"

Tally shrugged her pack higher on her shoulders and yanked on the brim of her felt hat. "I got bored. It's awful quiet there in the woods and lonesome."

"But you can't go now," Marc protested.

She tilted her head back and looked at him coldly. "Why not? I can do anything I want to. Nobody gives me any orders."

"I wasn't trying to give you orders." Marc fished the bag of cookies off the front seat and held it out to her. "What I meant was that I've barely gotten acquainted with you and I was hoping you'd stay around awhile so I could get to know you better."

"What do you want to get acquainted with me for?" Tally took a handful of cookies out of the bag and nodded her thanks. "I'm a pretty bad apple, you know. Back home respectable mothers considered me a bad influence on their children."

"You're the first honest person I've met."

"Oh, wow, what kind of people do you know?"

"He means you're the only person he's met he doesn't consider to be a hypocrite," Steve explained.

"Does he think you're a hypocrite?"

"Everybody's a hypocrite," Marc said. "Some people more than others. Even you and I, though we try hard not to be."

Tally took the last of the cookies and tossed the empty bag into the car. "Guess I'd better be on my way so I can get a ride before dark."

"Do you really want to go?" Steve asked.

"You got anything else to suggest?"

"Maybe Miss Tracey would let her stay with her," Marc said.

"Who's Miss Tracey?"

"She's a teacher in the social studies department."

"Some old maid who's been teaching forty years? No, thanks."

"Oh, no. She's real young. She's new this year. She's helping a bunch of us plan a demonstration on Mobilization for Peace Day."

"She's pretty radical." Steve smiled teasingly. "She's reported to have said in her classes that there are some good points about communism."

"That's radical?" Tally stared at him with her mouth open.

"Don't you think it is?"

"You must be kidding. Okay, I'll go see this Miss Tracey. If I don't like her I can pick up a ride in the center of town."

They all climbed into the car. "What do you do for fun in this place?" Tally asked as they drove back into town.

"Not much. There's the social center of Warton." Steve nodded toward an ice cream and sandwich restaurant on his left as he stopped at the red light at a four-way intersection. "Everybody checks in at Avery's at least once a day to see what's going on."

"Wow, some excitement. I think I'd just better keep going."

"See Miss Tracey before you decide." Steve pulled up before a shabby two-family house on a side street.

"Is this where she lives? Not a very fancy neighborhood."

"It's near the school," Marc said, "so she can walk. She sold her car to save money. She wants to go to Russia next year."

"I'll go up and get her." Steve opened his door. "There's no point in taking the whole Foreign Affairs club in on this before Tally makes up her mind."

Tally watched Steve stride up the walk. "He's a nice guy."

"He's about the best-liked guy in the school. That's why I'm glad he decided to help out on the peace demonstration. Lots of other kids will support it if he's in it."

"Doesn't sound to me as if your peace demonstration is a very popular idea."

Marc pressed his lips together. "The people in that high school are just like the rest of the people in this world, too interested in their own selfish affairs to care about the bigger issues."

"Here he comes. Is that Miss Tracey with him?"
Marc nodded.

"She doesn't look old enough to be a teacher."

Marc opened his door and climbed out. Miss

31

Tracey put her head and shoulders into the car and smiled at Tally. Tally leaned back and glared at her suspiciously from under her floppy hat brim. Miss Tracey sat down sideways on the front seat, crossed her arms on the top of the back, and gazed back at Tally. The two boys stood uneasily on the sidewalk.

"Why don't one of you say something?" Marc exclaimed.

"You got some other name besides 'Miss Tracey'?" Tally growled.

Miss Tracey stared at her unblinkingly. "Gwendolyn."

"You're kidding."

Miss Tracey shook her head. "I was named after a rich great-aunt."

"Then I suppose they tried to make up for that horror by giving you a cute nickname."

Miss Tracey nodded. "Wendy."

Tally made a face. "I always wished my name was Ann."

"So did I," Miss Tracey exclaimed. "Neat, short, and to the point."

"Right. And it feels good when you say it." Tally pushed back her hat and pulled her pack closer to her on the seat.

They gazed at each other some more, then Miss Tracey straightened, and delicately pushed her long straight hair behind her ears with her long fingers. "Okay?"

"For a couple of days, anyway. I never stay long in one place."

32

Miss Tracey pulled the front seat forward so Tally could slide out. Marc stared at her in surprise. "Is it all settled? You didn't say anything much. How do you know you'll like each other?"

Tally shrugged. "How do you know anything?"

"The whole Foreign Affairs club is sitting in my kitchen." Miss Tracey opened the front door and led the way up the dark, heavily varnished stairs. "Would you like to sit in on the meeting?"

Tally hung her pack strap over one arm and unzipped her khaki jacket. "Do you have a bathtub?"

Miss Tracey nodded.

"And lots of hot water?"

Miss Tracey nodded again.

"I guess I'll skip the meeting. You can tell me about it later." She followed Miss Tracey down the long, dark hall.

Marc and Steve went into the kitchen. "Hey, where you two been? We've been waiting for you for hours." A boy sitting at the table put down his soft-drink bottle.

"Have you made any plans?" Marc dropped his denim jacket on top of a pile of other coats and jackets near the door and sat down cross-legged on the floor. Steve leaned against the doorjamb and crossed his ankles and his arms.

"We can't decide whether to march all day or just for a couple of hours at noon."

"The town demonstration is just for an hour at noon. I think that's all we should do."

"I don't want to miss any classes."

34

"Maybe we could ask Mr. Johnson to give us credit for participating. After all, it is an historical event."

"I don't think he'd do that."

"Maybe we should ask for permission to go downtown and join the town march at noon."

"Or we could give people a choice, either join the school march or go down to the center."

"A lot of people would say they were going down to join the town march and then they'd go to Avery's or somewhere. Mr. Johnson wouldn't like that."

"Come on, gang, we've been over all this already. Make up your minds. I've got to go."

"What do you think we should do, Steve?"

Steve jerked his head toward his cousin. "Ask Marc. He's the president of this club and the demonstration was his idea in the first place."

"I know what Marc will say. He'll say we should all march all day up at the school."

Marc pushed himself to his feet and leaned against the enameled cast-iron sink. "That's right. You took the words out of my mouth."

"All day?"

"Suppose it's raining or snowing?"

"Or the wind's blowing? It's awful cold on that hill, especially by the flagpole where there's no protection."

"Suppose Mr. Johnson doesn't give us permission? Will you cancel the demonstration?"

Marc crossed his arms and vigorously massaged his elbows. "No, I won't. You all can do what you want to, but I'm going to march around the flagpole at the high school next Wednesday from eight in the morning until two in the afternoon regardless of the weather. I hope Mr. Johnson will give permission but if he doesn't I'm going to march anyway."

"Suppose he suspends you? He doesn't like having his orders disobeyed."

"He'll do what he thinks is right and I'll do what I think is right."

"Seems to me starting a war with Mr. Johnson isn't the best way to promote peace."

"Hey, we're here to make plans for a peace demonstration, not debate about civil disobedience."

"Well, I'm not going to march all day, no matter what Marc does."

"Marc's too much of an idealist."

Marc shook back his hair. "If you believe in something you should be willing to make some sacrifices for it, shouldn't you?"

"Everybody believes in peace."

"But nobody believes we can have peace now," Marc cried. "How long are we going to let the world pay lip service to peace and go on making war?"

"I don't see that my marching around the school flagpole even for a whole day is going to help one little bit to stop war. I don't start wars. It's the governments that start wars."

"If everybody in the world refused to fight in the wars the governments try to start, there wouldn't be any wars, would there?" Marc stuck out his chin and stared challengingly at the boy leaning against the refrigerator.

"You wouldn't go to war even if our country was attacked?"

"How could we be attacked if there was no one in any other country who would march off to attack us?"

The boy sitting at the table put his soft-drink bottle down with a clunk and stood up. "Marc, I love to listen to your utopian dreams but I've got to go. What about the peace march?"

The girl sitting beside him tapped the pad of paper in front of her with her pencil. "I gave up taking notes when you all started talking so fast. What'll I say in the letter to Mr. Johnson that we want to do next Wednesday?"

"Yeah, somebody make a motion. Then we can all vote and we'll all know what we're going to do."

The secretary pointed her pencil at Marc. "Make a motion. Only do it slowly so I can write it all down."

Marc tipped his head back and gazed at the cracked plaster ceiling. "I move that we ask Mr. Johnson for permission to invite the student body, the faculty, and the administration of Warton High School to participate in a march around the school flagpole from eight A.M. until two P.M. on Mobilization for Peace Day next Wednesday in order to join with other peaceful citizens all over the world in showing that we believe that 'peace now' as the goal of every nation should take precedence over every other national policy."

"This thing is worldwide?"

Marc pulled a much-folded letter out of the back pocket of his blue jeans and held it up. "That's what the organizing committee says in the letter I got suggesting our club join in."

Steve waved his hand and whistled. "There's a motion on the floor. Is there a second?"

"Second."

"Any discussions?"

"Are we going to carry signs?"

Marc nodded.

"Who's going to make them?"

Marc waved his arm around. "All of us."

"I'm awful busy. School play's in a couple of weeks."

"Let's settle the details later. How about voting on the motion?"

"Shall I read it again?" the secretary asked.

"No, no. Question. Question."

"Okay," Steve said. "All in favor, say 'aye.'"

There was a loud chorus of ayes. "All opposed, 'no.'" Nobody spoke.

"Good. Let's get out of here." In a few minutes only Marc and Steve were left in the kitchen.

"What do you suppose Tally and Miss Tracey are doing?" Marc went to the door of the kitchen and looked down the hall. "Miss Tracey?"

The door at the other end of the hall opened and Tally stuck her head out. "Is the meeting over?"

"Yes, we're going. Where's Miss Tracey?"

"We're busy," Tally said. "I'm trying on some of her clothes."

Miss Tracey's head appeared over Tally's. "What did you decide?"

"We voted to ask Mr. Johnson to let us have an all-day peace march around the school flagpole. Helen's going to write a letter and take it to him tomorrow."

"Will she give me a carbon of the letter?"

"I'll tell her to." Marc yanked his jacket out of the corner and put it on. "Thanks for having the meeting."

"That's all right. See you tomorrow in class."

"She sure tamed Tally down quick," Marc said to Steve as they walked down the front walk to the car.

"I wouldn't count on it. This may just be a lull before the storm."

"You think because she ran away from home she's bound to be a troublemaker?"

"She's not an ordinary girl."

"I think that's good. Ordinary girls are pretty boring. They never have any interesting ideas."

"You don't think some ideas can be too interesting?"

"Not for me."

# Chapter Four

"**H**ow'd you like school?" Marc asked Tally as they walked down the hill toward town.

"Honestly, I don't know why I bothered." Tally swung the tip of her long, flowing black cape up over one shoulder. "Hasn't anyone in this town ever seen a stranger before?"

"What happened? I didn't notice anything different."

"Every time I looked around someone was staring at me."

"You are pretty unusual-looking. Where did you get those boots with the big floppy cuffs? They look like something out of Shakespeare."

"Wendy had them in the back of her closet. She

40

wore them in a play in college. Aren't they cool?"

"And the cape?"

"Part of the same costume." Tally pushed up the brim of her hat and stared haughtily at the car full of boys, which raced by them honking.

"How come you decided to come to school today? Yesterday you said you weren't going to when Steve and I stopped around to see you."

"I got bored sitting around the apartment watching television. I have nothing against school as long as people leave me alone."

"Want to go to Avery's? I'm hungry."

"I'll have a cup of coffee."

A boy leaning against the parking meter in front of the sandwich shop straightened and whistled soundlessly at Tally as she swept through the door Marc was holding open. "You'd think I was painted green," she sputtered as she hung her cape on the hook at the end of the last booth in the shop.

"Sure you don't want anything besides coffee?" Marc asked.

She shook her head and sat down, sliding to the far end of the bench and leaning her head against the wall. Marc went up to the counter. "Hi, Paul. Two coffees, one black, one with cream, and two hamburgs. No, make it three hamburgs."

The boy in the white cap and dirty white apron behind the counter grinned at Marc as he threw three patties of meat on the grill and took the coffee pot off the hot plate. "What's the matter? Didn't you eat any lunch at school?"

"Are you kidding? Pork patties and gravy?"

Paul shoved the two full cups across the counter. "Hey, who's the girl? Everybody in school was talking about her today."

"She's a friend of Miss Tracey's." Marc carried the coffee to the booth and then went back for the hamburgs.

"I heard she's a runaway."

Marc shrugged. "You hear anything you want to, these days."

"Your sister was the one who said it."

"I never pay any attention to her." Marc stacked up the three small cardboard plates and carried them back to the booth.

"He was asking you about me, wasn't he?" Tally stirred her coffee vigorously. "Why can't people mind their own business?"

"How are you and Miss Tracey getting along?"

"All right. Only she has a lot of romantic ideas about making things better by using the political process."

"What's wrong with that?"

Tally stared at him. "Everybody knows it's too late for that. What we need is a revolution. And we're going to have it, too. You just wait and see."

"Revolutions don't accomplish a thing for the people who need help most. All they do is put a new elitist group in power."

"That's not so." Tally put her cup down with a crash on the saucer and leaned forward so the ends of her long hair swept the table. "If we had a revo-

42

lution in the high schools it would put the students in power and we're not an elitist group. We're the most downtrodden, mistreated group in this country."

Marc stopped chewing and stared at her. "You think we need a revolution in our high school?"

"You need something to get rid of that principal of yours."

"What's wrong with Mr. Johnson?"

"You should have heard all the nosy questions he asked me before he let me register. If Wendy hadn't been there I'd have told him a thing or two but she'd have been shocked. She has some idea I'm a nice girl."

"You are."

"My father didn't think I was."

"Marc, baby, mind if I share your booth?" A broad, heavy-set boy with short, wiry, crisp blond hair dropped into the seat beside Tally.

"Go away," she said without looking at him. "We're having a private conversation."

He leaned back and looked her up and down. "Ah, Miss Tally Dayton, the mystery girl. I've been hearing about you all day. My name's Frank Ventura. Pleased to meet you."

She turned her back on him and drained her coffee cup. "Come on, Marc, let's go."

"Not so fast there, honey. You interest me." Frank flicked a strand of her long red hair with his thumb and forefinger. "Is it true what I heard that you're a runaway that Marc and Steve dropped on Miss Tracey's doorstep like a stray cat?"

43

Tally's face turned red as she stared fiercely at the back of the seat across from her.

"Another thing I heard was that before you came here, you were living with a bunch of hippies and panhandling on the Common for bread until the cops told you to get out of town or they'd put you in jail."

"What I do is none of your business."

"Lay off, Frank," Marc said. "Come on, Tally."

As Tally started to get up Frank put his arm around her shoulders and pushed her down again. "Not yet, baby. I want to hear what it's like to run away from home."

"Why don't you do it and then you'll know." Tally pushed his arm off her shoulders. "Let me out of this booth."

"You're not going just when the conversation is getting interesting?"

"I certainly am." Tally scrambled up on the table. Frank caught her by the ankle.

"Come on back here. I haven't finished talking to you."

"Let go of me." Tally stamped hard on his wrist with the sharp wooden heel of her boot.

With a yelp of pain Frank leaped out of the booth, caught her with both hands, and dragged her off the table.

"Let go of her, Frank." Marc flung himself on Frank's shoulders, wrapping both arms tightly about his neck and kicking him as hard as he could on the backs of the legs.

44

Frank laughed. "Come on, Marc, fight like a man, not a baby." He let go of Tally and pried Marc's arms loose. Then, spinning around, he punched Marc hard in the face and sent him sprawling on the floor.

"You pig." Tally grabbed a cup in one hand and a saucer in the other and flung them at Frank.

Frank lunged at her. She dodged him, snatched up a sugar bowl, and hurled it. It hit him in the shoulder and sugar spilled out all over him. From one table to another she darted, grabbing up ashtrays, ice cream dishes, spoons, saltshakers, and glasses, flinging them at him in a steady stream. Frank dodged and lunged, his arms outstretched and his fingers working angrily. The other youngsters in the shop huddled as far out of the way as they could, forming a ring inside which Tally circled, her face pale and her breath coming in wheezing gasps.

Marc scrambled to his feet and leaned against a chair. One eye was already puffed up and his cheek was bruised. Moving stealthily from chair to chair, he edged up behind Frank. Desperately Tally dodged under Frank's outstretched arms. He spun and grabbed for her. Marc's leg shot out. Frank tripped and went down face first on the sticky, littered floor.

Marc fell on him, but before he could get a good grip on his short curly hair, Frank rose to his hands and knees and began to lunge from side to side, try-ing to shake Marc off. As Marc's hold loosened, Tally snatched up a banana-split dish and pounded Frank on the top of the head with it. Frank's lunges weak-ened.

45

"All right. All right. Quit it," he panted, raising one hand to ward off Tally's blows.

"You going to leave me alone?" Tally stood over him, the dish upraised.

Frank toppled Marc off his back and stood up, brushing the sugar off his shirt and wiping his sticky palms on his pants legs. He glared at Tally but didn't answer.

"Hey, here come the police." The crowd around the door moved aside. A policeman pushed into the shop. In the shadow of his visor, his eyes flicked around the long, narrow room. The huddled onlookers shuffled uneasily. Frank stared back at him defiantly. Tally set the banana-split dish down on a table, lifted her cape off the hook, and swung it around her shoulders. Beside her, Marc hunched over his folded arms and cradled his elbows in his hands.

"What's going on?" the policeman asked in a quiet, tired voice.

No one answered. Behind the counter, Paul ran his wet cloth over the stainless steel lids of the ice cream containers.

"Who called us?"

Paul lifted his chin as the policeman looked at him. "The place was getting busted up. I didn't think the boss would go for it."

"Who was busting it up?" There was a long silence. "You want to lodge any complaints against anyone?"

Paul shook his head.

46

The policeman kicked half of a broken saucer against the counter. "Who's going to pay for the broken dishes?"

"I am," Marc said.

The policeman looked at him closely. "What happened to you?"

Marc touched his cheek tenderly. "I ran into something."

"I guess you did. You don't look so good. Maybe I'd better take you home."

"I'm all right," Marc protested.

"Get your coat." The policeman waited while Marc shrugged into his denim jacket and then walked behind him out of the shop.

"Who's the girl with the red hair?" he asked as they cruised along in the police car.

"She's a friend of Miss Tracey's."

"The high school teacher?"

Marc nodded.

"What's her name?"

"Natalie Dayton."

"Where's she from?"

"Chicago."

"Relation of this teacher's?"

"I don't think so."

"What's she doing here?"

Marc shrugged.

The policeman turned into the Ainsworths' driveway. "Your mother home?"

"I guess so. Her car's here." They walked up the

flagstone walk together. Marc opened the door and stuck his head inside. "She's talking on the telephone."

"You go get her and tell her I want to speak to her."

Marc tiptoed down the hall to the kitchen. His mother was sitting on a low, white-painted metal stool with a flowered plastic cushion. Both elbows rested on the low white shelf littered with telephone books, pads, pencils, and pieces of paper. With her free hand she twisted and untwisted a strand of hair.

"Mom."

She turned her eyes toward him and gave a little scream. "No, Gladys, nothing's the matter." Quickly she covered the mouthpiece. "What happened to you?"

"Nothing. There's a policeman at the front door. He wants to see you."

"A policeman? What's he want? Is he selling tickets for the policemen's ball? Get two dollars out of my purse. It's on the counter." She uncovered the mouthpiece again. "Yes, Gladys, that's right. Everyone should have to do something. It isn't fair to make just a few of us in the club do all the work."

"Mom, he's not selling tickets."

"It's your father. He's had an accident." In her alarm she forgot to cover up the mouthpiece again. "What? No, Gladys, it's nothing. I'll call you back." She hung up and hurried ahead of Marc to the front door.

48

"Is it my husband?" she cried. "Has he had an accident? I've told him he drives that sports car of his too fast. Wait a minute and I'll get my coat and come with you."

"It's not your husband, Mrs. Ainsworth. It's your boy, here."

"Marc, what have you done?"

"It's obvious he's been in a fight, isn't it?" the policeman said a little impatiently.

"A fight? Where?"

"At Avery's."

"But he doesn't believe in fighting."

"We got a call to go to Avery's because there was a fight going on there. When I got there the place was a mess and your son had a black eye and a bruised cheek. Which he didn't get from drinking a cup of coffee and eating a hamburg."

"Oh, Marc, what will your father say? Will it be in the paper? My husband will be furious if it is. Are you going to arrest him?"

The policeman shook his head. "No, no complaint was made. I brought him home because he looked a little rocky to me and like he could use a ride instead of walking, and also because I wanted you and Mr. Ainsworth to be sure and know that Marc had been involved in a disturbance of the peace. Sometimes parents don't find out what their kids are up to until it's too late and they're in real trouble. That's all. Good night." The policeman nodded brusquely, turned on his heel, and strode down the walk to the police car.

Jean clutched Marc's arm. "Do you think we can keep your father from finding out?"

"It'll be a little hard, won't it, with my eye all swollen up and black?"

"Couldn't we say you ran into something?"

Marc laughed. "You think he'd believe that? Why do we have to lie to him?"

"You know what he's like when he gets upset."

"He'd be worse if he found out we were lying to him, wouldn't he?"

"I suppose so. Life is so complicated. Sometimes I could scream." She looked at her watch. "Oh, dear. It's later than I thought. I talked too long to Gladys. This garden club business is such a nuisance."

Marc followed her down the hall to the kitchen. "Why don't you give it up?"

"I can't do that. Your father wouldn't want me to. Some of the nicest women in town are in the club and being on the board is really an honor. But I do wish more of them would do some work and not just go to the meetings and stuff themselves at tea afterward."

"It doesn't sound honest to me. If I didn't like doing something, I'd stop doing it."

Marc took a banana out of a bowl on the shelf and wandered out of the kitchen. Jean's high voice drifted after him down the hall. "You just don't understand, Marc. You can't be honest with your father."

# Chapter Five

---

**S**O THE PEACENIK got into a fight." Budge forked a lamb chop onto a plate, dropped a baked potato beside it, put on a spoonful of peas, and passed the plate to Marc. "Tell me all about it."

Marc took the plate and put it down. "I'd rather not talk about it, Dad."

"I'll tell you about it," Sharon said excitedly. "I stopped in at Avery's with a bunch of kids just after it happened. You should have seen the place. Plates and cups and spoons and sugar and broken glasses and saltshakers all over the floor. It was a mess. We helped Paulie clean up and it took us three quarters of an hour."

"I thought this was a fistfight."

"Oh, no. Frank Ventura got fresh with this new girl and she told him to leave her alone and he wouldn't so she stomped on his hand."

"Stomped on his hand?"

"Yes, she was walking on the table to get out of the booth because he wouldn't let her go. That made him so mad he pulled her out on the floor, so Marc jumped on him and then he socked Marc and knocked him down and then this girl threw all those things at him to keep him from getting hold of her again."

"Frank Ventura, the football player?"

Sharon nodded.

"Who won?"

"Marc and the girl did, didn't you, Marc?"

"Nobody ever wins in a fight."

"Well, everybody said you won. Marc got up again and managed to trip Frank and get him down again, and then that girl began hitting him on the head with a glass banana-split dish until he gave up."

"The real reason he gave up is because the police came," Marc said.

"The police got in on this, too?"

"They assured me there wouldn't be anything in the paper about it," Jean said quickly. "No one was arrested."

"How did you get in on it?"

"The policeman brought me home," Marc said.

"He only did it because he thought Marc looked pale and shouldn't walk home. I'm sure nobody on the street saw the police car in the driveway." Jean smiled brightly around the table. "Why don't we talk about something else? Sharon, tell Daddy about your new dress for the country club dance."

"Later, later." Budge waved his hand impatiently and squinted at Marc in the dim light from the candles in the center of the table. "Are you all right? That's a beautiful shiner. You should be proud of it, son. Most people would think twice before taking on Frank Ventura."

"I suppose." Marc chewed gloomily on a mouthful of lamb chop.

"Who is this girl? She must be quite something if she can get Marc into a fight."

Sharon looked across the table. "You tell him, Marc. You know more about her than anybody. She's a real mystery girl, Daddy. She turned up in school today and nobody knows anything about her."

"Her name's Tally Dayton, she's from Chicago, and she's living with Miss Tracey. What's so mysterious about that?"

Budge smiled at Sharon. "Yes, honey, what's so mysterious about that?"

"There's more to her than that. Go on, Marc, tell Daddy where you met her."

Marc shook his head.

"Why don't you want to tell us about her, dear?" Jean looked hurt.

"Do you know where he met her?" Budge asked Sharon.

Sharon nodded and smiled triumphantly at Marc. "He and Steve saw her hitchhiking in the rain Wednesday and picked her up and let her spend the night in Mr. Barker's cabin on the river. That's why they wanted to leave your party so they could take her some food and a sleeping bag. Then, the next day, Marc persuaded her to stay with Miss Tracey because he didn't want her to leave."

"So the hermit is getting human at last." Budge winked at Jean. "I told you not to worry, honey. Sooner or later every boy gets interested in girls."

"But, Budge, hitchhiking? What kind of a girl would do that?"

Marc stared across the table at Sharon. "How did you find all that out?"

"One way and another. I told you you couldn't keep a secret from me."

"Why was she hitchhiking?" Budge demanded of Marc.

"Everybody hitchhikes these days."

"Nobody in this family hitchhikes."

"It's so dangerous for a girl," Jean murmured.

"I think she's a runaway," Sharon said.

"Oh, dear, how dreadful. What does she look like?"

"She's crazy-looking. Long, kinky red hair, big brown eyes, a real pale face, and weird clothes. Today she had on a short fringed skirt over tights, a black turtleneck jersey, boots with big floppy cuffs, a long flowing black cape, and a big floppy felt hat."

"She doesn't sound very attractive. Are you sure you want to go around with her, dear?"

"I'm not going around with her." Marc stared at his mother in exasperation. "I like her ideas. She's real. She's honest. She hates hypocrisy just the way I do. What difference do her looks make?"

"I wonder why she ran away."

"Maybe it was a more honest thing for her to do than to stay around and have to live a life she didn't approve of."

"Running away is cowardly," Budge said. "If you don't like the way things are, you should stick it out and try and change the situation, not run away from it."

"Suppose you have tried to change the situation and haven't had any success."

"I suppose you're implying this girl's parents are to blame for her running away. Kids nowadays are so ungrateful. I bet her parents gave her everything they could to make her happy, just the way your mother and I do for you and Sharon. And probably because they asked her to do some perfectly reasonable thing like wear shoes when she went downtown or turn down the record player or not smoke marijuana, she felt she had a right to run away."

"It doesn't seem right to me," Jean sighed. "Children should be home living with their parents."

Budge leaned forward in his chair and pulled his wallet from his back pocket. "If dishes got broken during that fight of yours, Marc, someone will have to pay for them."

"I said I was going to."

"I'd like to help out." Budge laid a twenty-dollar bill on the table cloth between him and Marc. "If that isn't enough, let me know."

"Thanks, Dad, but I can't take it. It was bad enough getting into that stupid fight. It would make it worse to let you bail me out of the consequences."

"There's nothing to be ashamed of in being in a fight if it's for a good cause. Sometimes you have to fight. Just the way we had to fight Hitler. There isn't any other way."

Marc pushed the bill back toward his father. "Thanks a lot. I really appreciate it but I can't take it."

"How are you going to pay for the dishes?"

"Paul says I can take his place for a couple of weeks behind the counter after school and he'll take a vacation with pay."

"What's happened to all your allowance?" Sharon asked. "You don't spend it all on food."

"Or on clothes." Budge wrinkled his nose in distaste as he looked at Marc's faded black jersey with the stretched neck and baggy sleeves.

"Yes, dear." Jean leaned forward, her arm outstretched on the table toward Marc. "You really must buy some decent clothes. The holidays are coming and there'll be parties and things and you can't wear your jeans and jerseys to everything."

"He gets fifteen dollars a week and all I ever see him spend money on is food." Sharon narrowed her eyes suspiciously. "What do you do with your allowance?"

"I send it all to CARE." Marc glared at her defiantly.

"You give away the money I give you every

week?" Budge cried. "I give you that money so you can hold your head up among your friends and never have to say you can't do something because you don't have the money. So you can clothe yourself decently, eat properly during the day at school, and have a little extra for some fun. And you give it away. Will you please tell me why?"

"He thinks your money is bloodstained, Daddy. He wrote a letter to the school newspaper a couple of weeks ago about the bloodstained money the American system rests on and told us not to spend it."

Budge swung around toward Marc. "What kind of talk is that?"

"Most of the money that's earned in this country is bloodstained, Dad. It either comes out of the sweat and deprivation of poor people, or it comes from making weapons with which our government supports repression all over the world, or it's made by manufacturing luxury goods which drain off the dollars which should go toward better housing, better schools, and better environment."

"In other words, the American system of capitalistic democracy which provides its people with the highest standard of living in the world is bloodstained through and through and should be thrown on the scrap heap." Budge leaned back in his chair and shook his head, laughing. "I give up, Jean. They say you should try and understand your children's point of view but I defy anyone to understand this one."

58

Jean looked puzzled. "You must get some money from somewhere, dear."

"I earn it doing odd jobs for the Miss O'Briens. That's where I've been going Saturdays."

Sharon bounced in her chair. "That's not fair. Now you'll probably pay his subscription to the country club dance and I'll have to pay mine out of my allowance."

"I'm not going to the country club dance."

"But you went last year, dear, and had a good time."

"I had a terrible time."

Jean looked troubled. "You said you had a good time. I remember you said it, because it made me feel so relieved to hear it since I was the one who urged you so strongly to go."

"You asked me how the dance was and I said it was all right. As dances go it was all right but that doesn't mean I had a good time."

"I think you'd better go this year," Budge said firmly.

"I don't want to, Dad."

"Now listen, Marc. Your mother and I joined the country club as much for you children as for ourselves, to give you a chance to meet some nice kids and have some fun. And as far as you are concerned, we might as well not have bothered. I have to order you to go over and play golf with me. You were in the pool twice last summer. You didn't go to any of the parties and you never pick up your tennis racket."

"I think country club living is immoral."

"Nothing immoral goes on at our country club. There may be a little flirting at dances but there certainly is nothing immoral."

"What about Lully Jones's mother and George Halborn's father?" Sharon asked.

"Good heavens, how did you hear about that?" Jean exclaimed.

"I mean it's immoral to spend all that money on pleasure when so many people in this world are dying of starvation."

"When a man works as hard as I do he deserves a little pleasure, especially when he's earned the money for it all by himself."

"Suppose you invited this girl, this Tally, that you like so much. Would you go to the dance then?" Jean smiled coaxingly.

"I wish you would, Marc," Sharon said. "I'd like to see what she'd wear."

Marc leaned back and folded his arms. "I'm not going to that dance."

Jean sighed. "I suppose I'd better call Shirley Larkin back and tell her not to count on you as an usher."

Sharon leaned across the corner of the table and smiled at her father. "Can I have that twenty dollars you were going to give Marc to pay for the broken dishes? Then I can take back the dress I bought for the dance and get the one I really wanted."

"Sure, honey." Budge pulled the bill out of his pocket and tossed it on the table near Sharon's plate.

"Thank heavens I have one child that's normal."

"Would anyone like dessert?" Jean jumped up. "It's blueberry pie. I discovered a new kind of frozen pie today. Velma recommended it to me so I thought I'd try one. You'd like a piece, wouldn't you, Budge?"

Budge threw out his arm and looked at his wrist watch. "Can't, honey. Haven't time. I have to be over at the club in fifteen minutes for the board of governor's meeting. Did you get my golf committee report typed up?"

"There are a few mistakes, I'm afraid. I had this problem with the garden club on my mind and didn't pay as much attention to the typing as I should have."

Jean hurried down the hall. As Budge followed her out of the dining room he tweaked a strand of Marc's shoulder-length hair. "If you really want to make time with that redhead you'll get that mop cut. Ideas are fine but looks count for more."

Marc hunched up his shoulders and didn't reply. Sharon clattered her dishes into a pile and stood up. "She probably likes his hair. It isn't any worse looking than hers." As she bounced out into the kitchen, the telephone rang. "I've got it," she yelled. "Hello? Oh, sure, just a minute." She dropped the telephone on the shelf, stamped through the dining room, and yelled up the stairs, "Mom, it's for you. It's Gladys."

After a few minutes, Jean hurried through the dining room with her coat on. "I've got to go over to Gladys's for a little while, dear. This garden club problem has to be settled before the club meeting tomorrow. I shouldn't be too late." She turned around in the kitchen door and looked at Marc anxiously. "You're all right, aren't you? After that fight, I mean?"

"Sure, Mom, I'm all right."

Jean hurried out the door to the garage. Marc leaned back in his chair and closed his eyes. Upstairs Sharon's radio played loudly. Once in a while she sang along with it. When the door chimes rang behind him in the hall he was almost asleep. Before he could get up to go to the door, Sharon ran down the stairs.

"I'll get it. Maybe it's that guy I was talking to at Avery's today." She flung open the door. "Oh, hello, what do you want? Marc, here's Tally." She let her in, pushed the door shut with a slam, and ran back upstairs.

"Your phone's been busy for half an hour," Tally said.

"I think the phone in the kitchen got left off the hook." Marc pushed himself to his feet and went out to hang up the receiver. "Good thing you came by," he said when he came back. "I was almost asleep."

"Let's go for a walk." Tally glanced up the stairs. "I don't want her to hear."

Marc got a long, heavy woolen overcoat out of the closet and pulled a knitted woolen hat down over his ears. He shut the big front door softly behind them and followed Tally down the walk.

She took his arm. "It's a beautiful night, isn't it?"

"It's cold. What did you want to talk about?"

"I want to be in your peace march."

"It's not my peace march. It's the school's. Anyone can be in it."

"Has the principal said it was all right to have it?"

"I haven't heard otherwise."

"That's bad."

"Why?"

"If the administration approves, it means you've been taken over by the establishment and are acting as their tools."

Marc stopped under a street light and looked at her in amazement. "We're not anybody's tools. We're exercising our right of free speech under the Constitution."

"Nobody is going to pay the least bit of attention to you."

"I don't care how much attention they pay to us. I'm doing this because I feel it's right for me to show how I feel about peace."

"Don't you want to make other people think about peace, too?"

"Sure."

"You won't unless you really get their attention."

"What am I supposed to do? Run around the flagpole naked with *Make love, not war* painted on me?"

"That's a good idea. Do you think it would make Mr. Johnson withdraw his permission for the march?"

"Do you want him to withdraw it?"

"Yes."

"You mean not have the march at all?"

"Of course not. That wouldn't do any good. I mean, have the march in spite of his refusal. Then people would really notice you."

"We'd get suspended. Mr. Johnson doesn't fool around when kids break the rules."

"It would be for a good cause, wouldn't it?"

"My father'd kill me if I got suspended."

"Are you scared of your father?"

"No, I'm not scared of him. We don't agree about most things but he's not a bad guy and I'd hate to hurt him."

"I bet he doesn't mind hurting you."

"I don't think he realizes what he's doing."

"I wouldn't stand for it."

"What am I supposed to do?"

"Run away."

"What good would that do?"

"It's the answer, man. If I'd stayed home and put up with all the stuff my parents were handing me I'd have gone insane. And you will, too, if you don't watch out. Parents don't have any right to treat their kids as if they were subhuman."

Marc caught Tally by the arm and pulled her onto the grass at the edge of the road. "There's a car coming."

The car stopped beside them and the driver leaned over and unwound the window on the passenger side. "Marc," Budge shouted, "what are you wandering around on the streets for at this hour of the night? Does your mother know you're out? Get in here right now and I'll take you home."

"Dad, this is Tally. We had something to talk about. Can we take her home?"

Budge pushed open the car door. Tally and Marc squeezed into the little back seat. "Couldn't what you had to talk about wait until tomorrow?" Budge asked as he shifted gears.

"No, it couldn't," Tally said.

"Why didn't you telephone?"

"Sharon left the kitchen phone off the hook," Marc explained. "The line was busy for half an hour."

"What did you have to talk about that was so important you had to come all the way over to our house in the dark and cold?"

"It's our business." Tally leaned back and wrapped her cape around her.

"I don't like my son having secrets from me."

"It was something about the peace march I'm organizing up at school," Marc said hastily.

"Peace march? More likely be a riot the way you kids do things these days. I don't want you mixed up in it."

"Dad, it won't be a riot."

"You stay out of it. How will it look to all my sales contacts in Washington if my son's mixed up in a peace protest?"

"You can't order him around like that," Tally cried.

"I can tell my son whatever I want, young lady." Budge stopped in front of Miss Tracey's house with a jerk. "Walk her to the front door, Marc, and make it quick. I'm tired."

"You aren't going to pay any attention to him, are you?" Tally cried as they hurried up the walk.

"I don't know," Marc said gloomily. "I didn't expect him to react like that." Budge honked the horn and gunned the motor. "I'd better go."

"She certainly isn't much to look at," Budge said as Marc slid into the front seat and slammed the door. "And she has absolutely no manners. I don't see what you see in her."

"I told you, Dad, I like her ideas."

"Well, I think she's a troublemaker and the sooner she goes back to where she came from the better off we'll be."

# Chapter Six

**H**OW MANY SIGNS will we need, Marc?" A boy standing at one end of the Ping-Pong table in Marc's basement dipped his brush in a jar of poster paint and held it poised over the piece of shiny white cardboard on the table in front of him.

"Yeah, how many people have signed up to march?" a girl at the other end of the table asked.

Marc looked up from the sign he was working on. "I don't know. I haven't asked Helen. She was in charge of the sign-up sheet."

"Where is the sheet?"

"In Miss Tracey's room."

Tally backed away from the table, holding her paintbrush up to keep the paint from dripping off the bristles. "How do you like that sign?"

The boy looked at it with his head tipped. "Is that red supposed to be drops of blood dripping off the words?"

Tally nodded.

"It's colorful," the other girl said. "Do you think it's peaceful?"

"It's supposed to be hinting at the alternative to 'Peace Now.'" Tally reached out and put another spot of red paint on the large piece of gray cardboard.

"Has Mr. Johnson said it was all right for us to have the march?" the boy asked.

"Helen hadn't had an answer from him by Friday afternoon."

"I don't think Helen is really very enthusiastic about this protest march. She could have gone in and asked him instead of writing a letter and sitting around waiting for him to write one back."

The girl at the end of the table threw down her brush and pushed back her long straight brown hair. "She is, too, John McCarthy. Only she has other things to do beside hang around Mr. Johnson's office and try and get in to speak to him."

John held up both hands soothingly. "Okay, Nancy. Don't get so excited."

Tally looked across the table at Marc as she held up her sign and blew on the wet paint to dry it. "Have you talked to your father anymore since last night?"

"I haven't had time. I never see him Saturday mornings. He has a nine o'clock tennis game at the indoor courts and I leave about then to go to work for my old ladies."

"Is your father thinking of joining the march around the flagpole?" Nancy asked.

"Ha," Tally exclaimed. "He told Marc he couldn't have anything to do with the march."

"Why did he do that?"

"He's afraid the other executives at United Products wouldn't like it," Marc said, "because it might be bad for the company. U.P. does a lot of work for the government, you know, and Dad thinks if they heard down in Washington that the son of a U.P. executive was in a peace demonstration they wouldn't give them any more orders for defense materials."

Nancy stood her sign up on the table and looked at it approvingly. "I'd like to think they'd hear about our march down in Washington, but I can't imagine they will."

"If the central committee has any luck at all organizing groups around the country and the world they may hear about it." Marc picked up a hammer and tacked his sign to a length of fresh white lath. "When it's all over I'm supposed to send them a report telling how many people marched and what the reactions were at school and in town."

"If you're not going to march, I'm not going to." John set his sign against a Lally column to dry and put a large piece of corrugated cardboard on the table. "In fact, if you don't march, we might as well call the whole thing off since it was your idea."

"I think that's pretty awful of your father," Nancy said. "I was mad because I couldn't get my mother to say she'd go down to the center of town and stand around the flagpole for an hour but this is even worse. What right has your father got to interfere with your expressing your opinions on an important thing like peace?"

"It's not as if it was going to be a big demonstration." Tally put another spot of red paint on her sign. "We'll be lucky if half the people in the school realize what's going on."

John tapped his piece of cardboard with the eraser end of the pencil with which he had been outlining letters. "Well, how about it, Marc? Are you going to march or aren't you? There's no point in my making another sign if we're not going to have the protest."

Marc hunched his shoulders over his crossed arms and caressed his elbows while he stared at the sign lying in front of him. "Yes," he sighed after a long silence, "I'm going to march."

"Good." Tally seized the hammer and a piece of lath and vigorously nailed her sign to the stick. "Now we can get serious about this thing."

Upstairs a door slammed and heels clicked over their heads on the kitchen floor. "Marc?" Jean's high voice echoed through the basement. "Are you there? I just came back from my luncheon and I want you to come downtown with me to buy some new clothes."

"Mom, I'm busy. Can't we do it some day after school?"

"I can't do it any afternoon next week, dear, and Thanksgiving is almost here so we must get it done."

Marc laid down his brush and went to the foot of the cellar stairs. "Mom, I've got some kids here and we're right in the middle of something. I can't leave now."

Jean clattered halfway down the stairs and smiled brightly at the group around the table. "What is it you're doing?"

"We're making signs." Marc pointed from one person to another with the end of his paintbrush. "Mom, this is Tally and that's John and that's Nancy." The youngsters ducked their heads and murmured politely.

"I'm glad to meet you all, too." Jean smiled again. "I'm sorry I have to take Marc away, but you can all stay and go right on with what you're doing. He may be back before you're finished. We only have to get him a pair of trousers and a couple of shirts and a nice jacket. And he's not fussy, you know, about his clothes, so I don't think it will take us long."

Tally shook back her hair. "What's the matter with the clothes he has?"

Jean stared at her in surprise for a moment and then laughed. "He has a very critical grandmother who notices everything her grandchildren do and doesn't hesitate to point out the things she doesn't approve of."

"You ought to tell her to mind her own business."

Tally stirred her jar of poster paint briskly with her brush and bent over a fresh piece of cardboard.

Jean's eyes widened. Then she looked at Marc with a troubled frown. "Come on now, dear, don't make things any harder for me. You know how your father feels about the clothes you wear. If we don't do something soon about them he will really scold us."

She smiled at John. "Do you have trouble with your father, too, over your clothes and the length of your hair?"

John shook his head and shrugged with an embarrassed smile. "Sometimes, I guess. Everybody does."

Jean stamped her heel on the stair and turned around. "Come on, Marc. I don't have much time. Daddy and I have to go to a cocktail party later this afternoon and out to dinner after that."

Marc dropped his brush into a glass of water, looked at his friends, and, without a word, tramped heavily up the stairs after his mother.

In the dim, crowded, high-ceilinged men's clothing store he stood squeezed up against a rack of suits while Jean and a clerk sorted through a rack of sports jackets.

"What was the size of your last jacket, Marc?"

"I don't know, Mom. I've forgotten."

The clerk held up a jacket. "Let's try this one on for size."

Marc dropped his long overcoat on the floor and

73

let the clerk slide the jacket up over his arms and settle it across his shoulders. "That looks about right. How do you like it, sonny?"

"It's all right."

"I thought you didn't like blue," Jean said.

"I don't care, Mom. Any color's okay."

"How about this one?" Jean held up a brownish tweed.

"That's the wrong size," the clerk said. "How about this one?" He pulled a dark green tweed jacket off the rack.

"That's better than that blue one. Try it on, Marc." Jean pulled the blue jacket off him, handed it to the clerk, and helped him into the green one.

"How does that one feel?" the clerk asked.

"Fine."

"Fits all right?"

Marc nodded.

"We'll take it," Jean said. "What kind of pants do you want to go with it, Marc?"

"I imagine he wants corduroy," the clerk said. "That's what all the boys are wearing these days."

"You don't think charcoal-gray flannel would be better for parties and dress-up occasions?" Jean wrinkled her forehead doubtfully.

The clerk shook his head. "No one under forty wears gray flannels these days. What size pants?"

Marc shook his head. The clerk pulled a tape measure off a hook on the wall and encircled Marc's waist, then measured the inside of his leg. "Thirty-one, thirty-one. You're as wide as you are high, sonny."

74

"I tell him he shouldn't eat so much. It must be all those snacks after school at Avery's." Jean smiled confidingly at the clerk as he looked over the piles of pants on the counter, then lifted the top half of a pile of light-tan corduroy pants and whipped out a pair.

"Want to take these in back and try them on?"

"I don't like that color."

"What color would you like, dear?" Jean laid her hand on a pile of dark brown pants. "How about this?"

"I don't think we have his size in those." The clerk looked at the tags stapled to the tops of the pants. "Here's your size in dark green."

"They'd look nice with your new jacket," Jean said. "Why don't you try them on?"

"I don't need to try them on." Marc took the pants from the clerk and handed them to his mother. "Here. Now let's go home."

"We have to get some shirts first."

"What size?" the clerk asked.

"I wear a medium jersey," Marc said.

The clerk sighed and pulled the tape measure down again. "Fifteen, thirty-two." He turned around and looked at the piles of shirts on the shelves. "I don't have much in that size. It's a popular one." He laid a fan of shirts in plastic bags on the counter. "Any of these colors would look good with that jacket and pants."

"This pale gold one is pretty." Jean held the packaged shirt under Marc's chin. "And that color becomes you, too."

"I think I'd like white, Mom."

The clerk gathered up the shirts, put them back on the shelf, and pulled down a white one. "Anything else?"

Jean looked longingly around the crowded store. "Wouldn't you like a nice wild necktie?"

"I've got two ties already."

"How about a sweater? They have some lovely ones."

"I have one I like, Mom."

"I guess that's all then. I'd thought of getting him a new coat but it's so hard to buy clothes for someone who isn't the least bit interested in how he looks."

The clerk opened his sales book. "Cash or charge?"

"Charge."

As they were driving home Jean patted the pile of packages on the seat between them. "Do me a favor, dear, and show what we bought to Daddy. It pleases him so to have us appreciate his providing us with nice things."

"Mom, I didn't ask him to buy me all this stuff."

"Honestly, Marc, couldn't you once in a while think about somebody besides yourself. It seems as if you go out of your way to be difficult."

"If you and Dad would just leave me alone everything would be all right. You're always trying to make me do things your way. Nobody tries to understand how I feel about things."

"We do try to understand but your ideas are so strange. Every time you and Daddy talk he ends up all upset and irritated."

"Everything seems to irritate him these days."

"He's under tremendous pressure at the office. I guess that's the penalty a man pays for being successful. And now there's talk of United Products acquiring another company which might mean a shake-up in the management and spoil his chances of moving up higher in the company. He'll be so disappointed if that happens."

"That's a pretty selfish, materialistic goal for a man to live for."

"I never thought about it that way. I think he's doing it for us because he loves us and wants us to have nice things and a comfortable life."

"What's the good of all the things if nobody's happy? I remember when we used to have fun with Dad. When we'd go off in the canoe, the four of us, for a picnic up the river. Or play croquet Sunday afternoons in the back yard, or cards in front of the fireplace in the winter. Now you're both so busy all the time."

"You wouldn't want to do those things now you're so grown-up, would you?" Jean turned into the driveway and parked her station wagon beside Budge's little car. "Good, Daddy's home. Come with me while I show him your new clothes. Maybe you'd even try on the jacket for him."

Budge was sprawled on the living room sofa reading a magazine. He sat up when Jean and Marc came in, dropped his magazine, and swallowed the last of the drink in the tall glass on the coffee table.

"We've been shopping, dear." Jean put the paper

bags on a chair and took off her coat. "Show Daddy what we bought, dear, while I hang up my coat."

"You said you'd do it," Marc muttered.

Jean looked at him sternly, gave a little jerk with her head toward the packages, and left the room. "Well, so you got some new clothes." Budge went over to the bar table between the windows and refilled his glass. "That's great. Let's see what you bought."

Marc picked up one bag after another by the bottom and dumped their contents onto the chair. The shirt in its slippery plastic bag slid onto the floor and the jacket fell in a heap on top of the still-folded pants. Jean hurried back into the room, picked up the shirt, and laid it on the coffee table.

"I tried to get him to buy a pretty colored shirt like some of yours, dear, but he wanted white." She shook out the jacket and held it up. "Here, Marc, try it on so Daddy can see how nice you look."

Budge nodded. "That's great. I expect it'll look even better when he's wearing something besides blue jeans and that jersey."

"Aren't these pretty?" Jean held the green corduroy pants up to Marc's waist.

Budge nodded again. "You lose a little weight around the middle, buddy, and you'll look sharp as a tack."

Jean pulled Marc's hair out from under the collar of the jacket and yanked on it playfully. "And maybe, Budge, if we say pretty-please-with-sugar-on-it he'll get a haircut before your mother comes for Thanksgiving."

Marc thrust his chin out stubbornly and stared past her without answering.

"I'll never understand you kids." Budge shook the ice in his glass. "Why is it you go out of your way to make yourselves look homely and unattractive? When I was your age I was always making sure I looked my best. Of course, we didn't think much of the guys who carried combs around in their shirt pockets and were always combing their hair, but we'd rather have been caught dead than be seen in the rags you kids wear everywhere."

Marc took off the jacket and dropped it on the chair. "Clothes are hypocritical. People use clothes to make themselves seem better than other people and to help themselves get ahead by impressing the people who run the system."

"You think we should all wear uniforms like the Nazi storm troopers?"

Marc folded his arms and squeezed his elbows. "Maybe we should all go naked."

Budge threw himself back onto the sofa and put his glass down so hard the ice tinkled. "Why is it every time I try to have a serious conversation with you all I get is foolishness?"

"But, Dad, I am serious. If no one wore any clothes then everyone would be judged for what they are and what they can do, not for the kind of façade they put on."

"You don't think people have a social obligation to those around them to try and look the best they can?"

"But then you get into the problem of judging

what's the right thing to wear. And usually it's those on top in the system who decide what should be worn, and they put down anyone who doesn't wear what they say is right."

"How far do you think I'd get in business if I went to work in sandals and ragged bell bottom pants and an African shirt with a lot of beads dangling around my neck? Dressed like that, how many orders would I have gotten in the days when I was a salesman on the road?"

"Was it your clothes that made you a good salesman or was it you?"

"The clothes helped as you'll find out one of these days when you try and get a job."

"Any employer I work for is going to have to be more interested in me and what I have to contribute to his business than he is in my clothes."

Budge snorted. "And how is this mythical employer supposed to tell what you have to contribute if you don't have a few externals like proper clothes, a degree from a good college, and some good references to give him a clue?"

"If he can't tell from talking to me what I'm like then I don't want to work for him."

"And I'm sure he isn't going to want you to work for him." Budge reached for his glass and stood up. "I'm going to get dressed. We'll leave for the Mac-Intyres' in half an hour?"

Jean nodded. When he had left the room she handed the new clothes to Marc. "Take these to your room and hang them up. And tomorrow you're going to wear them to church. Is that understood? And there'll be no more talk in this house about people going around naked either." She hurried out of the room, her heels leaving tiny dimples in the pile of the oriental rug.

# Chapter Seven

J EAN, LOOK AT THIS." Budge tramped into the
kitchen with the first section of the Sunday newspaper
in his hand.

"What is it, dear? I can't see." Jean peered over
his elbow at the paper while she continued to stir the
gravy she was making in the roasting pan. A piece
of roast beef steamed on a platter on the shelf beside
the stove, and mashed potatoes and green beans bub-
bled in pans on the back burners.

Budge thumped the front page with the tip of his
index finger. "It says here that some organization
called Mobilization for Peace has presented ultima-
tums to several businesses in the area which have
government defense contracts, demanding that they
publicly announce by Wednesday, Mobilization for

Peace Day, that they will immediately give up their government contracts or else this organization will picket them all day Wednesday and call for a boycott of all their products which are sold to the public. One of the companies they are threatening is United Products. What do you think of that?"

"Excuse me, dear, I want to get a strainer out of that drawer you're standing in front of."

"Isn't that the most ridiculous thing you ever heard?"

Jean put the strainer on the top of a pitcher and lifted the roasting pan. "You'd better move a little more, dear, or I'll bump your sleeve with the edge of this pan when I pour the gravy and it's probably greasy."

Budge moved a little and shook the paper. "It says this organization is calling for a worldwide demonstration on Wednesday for peace. I wonder how many people they'll be able to get out in Russia or Red China."

Jean put the roasting pan down and picked up the saucepan of potatoes. "Wasn't the minister talking about some kind of a demonstration here in Warton on Wednesday around the town flagpole at noon?"

"I didn't hear the sermon if you recall. I was helping Gordon count the collection."

Jean put down the empty potato pan and spooned the beans into a bowl. "He urged us all to come down and participate in the demonstration. He said peace is an idea we must all actively affirm if we ever expect to have it on earth."

"I wish he'd preach a good old-fashioned sermon once in a while on something out of the Bible, instead of always pushing us into social action."

Jean untied her apron. "Everything's all ready. Would you carry in the roast, dear? Sharon, Marc, dinner's ready."

Budge tucked the newspaper under his arm and picked up the platter. Jean followed him into the dining room with the bowl of green beans in one hand and the bowl of potatoes in the other, and then hurried back for the gravy. "Oh, Marc," she exclaimed as she sat down, "you changed your clothes already. I was hoping you'd wear them for Sunday dinner, too."

"Tally and I are going for a walk this afternoon. I'm supposed to be at her house in three quarters of an hour."

Budge looked up from carving the roast. "I was going to be home this afternoon and I thought you and I could work on your application for admission to Yale."

"What application?"

"I guess I forgot to tell you. When I sent the alumni office a notice about my promotion, I asked them to send me the application forms for you to look at. They came to the office Friday and I brought them home in my briefcase.

"It's too soon to think about it."

"It's never too soon to think about an important thing like that."

"But I don't want to go there anyway."

"Of course you do. It's one of the best colleges in the country. And being the son of an alumnus should give you a little advantage."

"My marks aren't the greatest, you know."

"You're in the top fifth of your class."

"There are still plenty of guys ahead of me."

"We'll give it a try anyhow. You never can tell."

"I'm not even sure I want to go to college at all."

"You've said that before and I'm not even going to listen. You're going to college and that's that."

"But why, Dad?"

"What do you think you're going to do if you don't go to college?"

"I want to learn to do something with my hands. Carpentry or cabinetmaking or even plumbing or electrical wiring. Something more fundamental and useful than working in an office."

"You work with your hands? Why, you're as clumsy as a puppy. Look at the way you fall all over yourself on the tennis court."

"He made me a lovely little stool in his junior high wood-working course," Jean said. "I still have it, too."

"There's no money in cabinetmaking."

"I'm not interested in money, Dad. I just want to get some satisfaction out of what I'm doing."

"I'm sure you'll get a lot of satisfaction out of your fellow carpenters and electricians and plumbers. They'll be such stimulating intellectual companions."

"How many people do you know at United Products who are intellectually stimulating?"

"At least I can count on them not to eat their peas with their knives if I invite them to the house for dinner."

"Remember the little man who came last winter to weather-strip the new kitchen door, dear?" Jean leaned on her elbows and peered down the table at Budge. "He was the most contented, cheerful person I've ever talked to. He had a house and some land in the country and he and his wife fed the birds and had such a nice time. I don't suppose you'd call him intellectually stimulating but he was very interesting to talk to. He told me right off without even seeing it that the bird I couldn't seem to find in my bird book was a tufted titmouse."

"And I suppose when you're over at the country club playing golf or eating lunch with Gladys Wells or Eugenia MacIntyre or some of the other ladies and they ask you what Marc is doing, you're going to be really proud to say, 'Oh, he's weather-stripping kitchen doors or building kitchen cabinets or putting the pipes in someone's new bathroom'?"

"But, Dad, it's my life. I think I should decide what I'm going to do with it."

"How do you know what decisions to make? You don't know anything about life."

"It's not my fault. You've kept me too sheltered in nice, middle-class, white suburbia all these years and I'm tired of it. I'd like to leave home tomorrow and go live in the city and get a job."

"Oh, Marc, you mustn't do that," Jean cried.

"I wish he would." Sharon jabbed her fork into her

mashed potatoes and stirred them vigorously. "He does nothing but embarrass me at school with the horrible way he looks and the stupid things he does. Letters to the editor and then that fight at Avery's over that girl and now this stupid peace march he's organizing."

"Peace march?" Budge stared blankly at Sharon for a moment. Then his face cleared and he turned toward Marc. "I thought I told you the other night you couldn't have anything to do with that."

"Dad, I can't back out now. Everything's all arranged."

"Has Mr. Johnson said it was all right?"

"I expect we'll know Monday."

"You don't need to worry, Daddy," Sharon said. "Hardly anybody is going to participate. Just a few people who are as weird and way-out as Marc."

"Will your demonstration at the school have any connection with the one Reverend Cumberland mentioned this morning in his sermon?" Jean asked.

"We're all part of the same thing. Mobilization for Peace Day. It's an international observance."

"You're part of that?" Budge reached down for the newspaper lying beside his chair. "You're part of that group that's going to picket United Products on Wednesday unless we give in to their ridiculous demand that we give up all our government contracts?"

"I didn't know they were going to do that."

"Well, they are. It says so right here on the front page." Budge thrust the paper at Marc.

"I'm glad somebody's speaking out about all the defense-related industries in this area."

"Well, that somebody isn't going to be you. Is that understood?"

"Dad, that's not fair."

"Neither is it fair for a man who works as hard as I do for his family to have his son constantly criticizing him and undermining his efforts."

"I'm not criticizing you, Dad. It's United Products I don't like."

"What's the difference? A man's work is his life. I'm not going to let you destroy the position I've worked so long and hard to build up."

"Sometimes you have to put ideals before your own selfish interests."

"I did that once in my life. I took three years out of my life right at the most crucial time to go and fight for my country and the ideals it stands for. It wasn't easy to come back, finish college, find a job, and catch up with all the draft dodgers and youngsters who didn't have to fight. I'm not going to let anything happen now that will make me slip behind again."

"You had your chance to stand up for your ideals. It's only fair to give me a chance to stand up for mine."

"Not at my expense."

"I don't think anyone at United Products will ever know that I took part in this demonstration at the school. You heard Sharon say there are only a few of us who are going to march. Hardly anyone is interested."

Budge reached out and tapped the newspaper with the toe of his shoe. "If your march is tied up with the group which is threatening to picket us on Wednesday they're bound to hear about it."

"I can't believe they'd really care, dear," Jean said.

"Listen, I'm the one who works there and I know how they'd feel. Marc is not to take any part in any peace demonstration on Wednesday. Do you hear?"

Marc nodded.

"Promise me you won't march."

Marc doubled up over his folded arms and stared at his plate.

"Promise me," Budge shouted.

Marc shook his head. "I can't, Dad."

Budge jumped up, came around the table, and pulled Marc out of his chair. "Promise me or you'll spend the rest of the day in your room."

"No, Dad, I won't."

Budge dragged him by the arm out into the hall and pushed him toward the stairs. "You get up in your room and you stay there until I tell you you can come out." He stood at the foot of the stairs, his hands on his hips, and watched Marc drag up the stairs and into his room.

An hour or so later Sharon flung open Marc's door. "Daddy wants you downstairs in the cellar. Quick."

Marc closed the book he was reading and sat up on his bed. "Why?"

"He found those signs you all were making yesterday for the peace march."

Marc sighed resignedly and followed Sharon downstairs, through the kitchen, and down the cellar stairs. Budge was standing over the pile of signs lying on the Ping-Pong table.

"Did you make these?"

"Some other kids helped."

"Yesterday?"

"Yes."

"After I'd told you the night before you weren't to have anything to do with that demonstration?"

Marc nodded.

"You deliberately disobeyed me."

"I suppose you could call it that."

"And what would you call it?"

"Standing up for my rights as an individual human being."

"Your rights." Budge pushed the pile of signs and sent the top one sliding to the floor. "As long as you live in my house, eat the food and wear the clothes I provide, you don't have any rights except the ones I give you."

"I have the right to follow my own conscience."

"Don't argue with me. You take those signs upstairs right now and burn them in the fireplace, sticks and all."

Budge stood back and watched while Marc gathered the signs into his arms and then followed him up the stairs and through the house to the living room. When Marc had torn the signs off the sticks, laid

Wharton Sunday News Ti...

MOBILIZATION FOR PEACE
ULTIMATUM TO LOCAL
BUSINESSES IN AREA

MOBILIZATION FOR PEACE

...OTT OF PLEDGES

...UNITED PRES...

them in the fireplace, and broken the laths in halves and laid the pieces on the signs, Budge threw him a box of matches and then sat down in an armchair, leaned back, rested his chin on his folded hands, and watched the flames curl the edges of the heavy pieces of paper. Marc stayed on his knees in front of the fireplace. Neither of them moved when the doorbell rang.

"I'll get it." Sharon, who had been standing in the hall watching, flung open the front door. "Marc, here's Tally."

Tally swept into the living room, her cape floating out behind. "I thought we were going for a walk."

Marc turned around slowly and stared at her.

"What's the matter? What are you burning? Are those our signs?"

"Yes, they are, young lady." Budge rose out of his chair. "The other night you heard me forbid Marc to take part in that peace demonstration. You shouldn't be surprised to find out I meant what I said."

"Those signs don't belong to you. They belong to us. You have no right to burn them."

"Rights. Rights. Rights. You kids today talk an awful lot about your rights. It would be nice if you'd think as much about other people's rights."

Tally turned on Marc. "Why did you give in to him? Are you afraid of him? He can't do anything to you."

Marc stood up and dusted off his knees. Behind him the flames roared up the chimney as all the cardboard caught fire. Tally flung out her arm. "Look at that.

A whole afternoon's work wasted because you didn't have the guts to stand up to him. I suppose you're going to back out of the demonstration, too."

Marc shook his head. "No, I'm not."

"Now, listen here, young lady." Budge advanced on Tally, his arm outstretched. "I never had any trouble with Marc until you came along. You get out of here and stop giving him ideas."

Tally sidestepped around Budge. "He had plenty of ideas before I came along, didn't you, Marc? Only before he didn't have the courage to stand up for them."

"If you were my child I'd take you over my knee and give you a good spanking."

Tally leaned forward until her hat brim brushed Budge's forehead. "Go on, try it. I dare you."

Budge grabbed her shoulders, spun her around, and marched her double quick to the front door. Still keeping hold of her with one hand, he turned the knob with the other, pushed her out onto the doorstep, slammed the door, and locked it. As he turned around, Tally pushed open the mail slot and yelled through it, "Right on, Marc, right on. Don't give in. He can't hurt you. Remember, you can always run away."

# Chapter Eight

W HAT DID HE SAY, MARC?"

"Did he say why he hasn't told us yet if we can march?"

"What took you so long in the office?"

Marc dropped his pile of school books on one of the front desks of the classroom where half a dozen boys and girls were waiting for him, lounging at the desks, doodling on the blackboard, or reading. Tally dropped the piece of chalk with which she had been drawing designs on the blackboard ledge and turned around.

"Yes or no? Here it is Tuesday afternoon and we don't know yet."

Marc pushed back his hair from his temples with the palms of his hands. "It's yes and no."

"What's that mean?" John flung the magazine he had been reading back on the bookshelf.

"Yes, we can march. No, we can't march all day. Only for the first class period. We can have only one sign and it can only say *Peace* and nothing else. And only members of the Foreign Affairs club can march. And if anything more happens between now and tomorrow morning permission is withdrawn for the whole thing."

"Anything more? What's happened so far?"

"He's had some letters from people in town objecting to the march."

"I didn't think anybody in town knew about it," Helen said.

"How many letters has he had?"

"Four or five. A couple of them were real violent. One accused him of preferring to be red than dead, and another one said if he allowed the march he wasn't fit to be principal and ought to be fired. The others just said the march was unpatriotic and a desecration of the flag and a waste of expensive learning time and stuff like that."

"Were any of them signed?"

Marc shook his head.

"Then he shouldn't pay any attention to them," John said. "Everyone knows that anonymous letters come from crackpots and shouldn't be taken seriously."

"Well, he's taking them seriously." Marc perched on one corner of the teacher's desk. "The one about better red than dead was written in red ink. And the one about how he should be fired had a drawing in the lower corner of a man getting his head chopped off with an ax."

"It sounds fantastic." Tally stopped pacing slowly back and forth in the space between the blackboard and the front row of desks and leaned with both hands on the other end of the teacher's desk. "Did you see these letters?"

"Yes, he showed them to me."

"You don't think he wrote them himself in order to have an excuse to clamp down on the demonstration?"

"Oh, Tally, Mr. Johnson wouldn't do a thing like that," Helen protested.

"How do you know he wouldn't? He thinks he has authority over us, doesn't he? And when people think they can tell other people what to do, they get funny ideas."

"I know Mr. Johnson. If he didn't want us to march he would have come right out and told us so." Nancy came down to the front of the room and sat on top of one of the desks. "He doesn't fool around being subtle."

"Maybe he used to be like that, but are you sure he still is? People who are on the side of the establishment have found out lately what happens when they come right out and say what people can do and can't do. I think he's against our demonstration only he's scared to come right out and say so for fear we'll riot or do something to destroy his precious school property, so he dreamed up those letters as an excuse for limiting us."

"At least he's letting us march."

"For one hour with one sign and only a handful of people." Tally tossed her head scornfully. "What kind of a protest demonstration will that be?"

"What do you think we should do?" a boy in the back of the room asked.

Tally walked up close to a front desk, leaned on its top with both hands, and stared intently at the questioner. "I think we should have a revolution."

"Are you kidding?"

"Be serious."

"Tally, you're crazy." Marc hopped off the corner of the teacher's desk. "You don't have a revolution until things are so bad there's nothing else to do but tear down the whole structure and start over again."

Tally spun around and faced him. "Don't you think things are bad around here now? I do."

"What's wrong with our school?" John said belligerently. "We've got the most liberal dress code of any school around. Look at Marc. He couldn't come to school looking like he does anywhere else and neither could you."

Tally snorted scornfully. "Dress codes. That's kid stuff. Why do you think administrations raise all this fuss about what kids wear and how long your hair is and whether you have beards or not? Because they care how we look?" She snorted again. "It's to keep our minds off the real shackles they've got on us."

"It would be nice if we had more say about the curriculum," Nancy said.

Tally waved her hand impatiently. "That's secondary. I'm talking about personal freedom. The school authorities can make any rules they want and we have no way to fight back. Look at our peace demonstration. It's our idea. It's our ideals we want to express and yet Mr. Johnson can tell us exactly how we must do it and if we don't like it there's nothing we can do."

"That's right. If we don't do what he says, out we go." John slapped the top of the desk he was sitting at.

"See what I mean?" Tally shouted triumphantly. "First they pass a law that says we have to go to school. Do they ask us if we want to go to school? No, they tell us we have to go because they say it's good for us. Then, if they don't like the way we act they can toss us out. But do they let us stay out if we want to? No, they send attendance officers around after us just as if we were criminals. That's the kind of thing it will take a revolution to change."

"But, Tally," Helen protested. "We can't go around ignorant. We have to learn to read and write and things."

"Why do I have to come to school to learn that? I can study just as well at home and not have to waste my time listening to a lot of dumb kids and dumb teachers droning on. They herd us into these prisons they call schools because they're scared of what we might do to the power structure if they let us into the real world, not because they want us to learn anything."

John leaned back in his chair and looked at Tally with respectful eyes. "Yeah, that's right. I forget everything I learn right after the quizzes because I never do anything with it."

"I don't see what all this talk has to do with our demonstration tomorrow." Nancy stacked up her books and started to put on her coat. "I've got to go. Jerry'll be through practice in a few minutes and I don't want to miss my ride home."

"I think we should turn the demonstration tomorrow into a confrontation with the administration." Tally stood up tall and banged her left palm with her right fist. "I think we should march all day, or until he stops us by force. I think we should have a sign for everyone and I think we should recruit all the kids we can to march, whether they're interested in peace or not."

"You go ahead if you want to, but one hour is all I want to march and I won't have time before tomorrow to make another sign." Nancy pulled on her gloves and popped the hood of her coat up over her head. "So long. I'll see you at the flagpole at eight. I'll ask Jerry if he wants to march, but I doubt it. He's not much interested in anything right now except basketball."

"Tally, this demonstration is for peace." Marc's chubby face was troubled. "What does a confrontation with Mr. Johnson have to do with it?"

She wheezed with exasperation. "The demonstration is only a pretext. What we're really interested in is the deeper issue of more power for the students. His putting all those restrictions on the demonstration is perfect. If we play it right, we can make him look like a bigger fascist than Franco and really get this place liberated."

"You've lost me."

"Me, too." Two of the boys who had been leaning against the bookshelves in the back of the room walked toward the door.

"You'll be at the flagpole at eight, won't you?" Marc asked them anxiously.

"Sure, but only for an hour."

"I don't really think I'm interested in student power, Tally." Helen picked up her coat from the desk top behind her, hung it over her arm, and gathered up her books. "Peace is something I really care about but I don't want to fight with Mr. Johnson. I think he's nice."

"You'll march tomorrow?" Marc followed her to the door.

"For an hour, but if it looks as if it's going to turn into a fight I'll leave. I hate it when people start getting rough."

"What about you?" Tally whirled around and looked at John fiercely.

He yawned and stretched. "You've got a lot of interesting ideas, Tally, but I'm not into student power and revolution and all that. It takes too much energy." He pushed himself out from behind the desk, picked up the one book he had with him, and

100

sauntered to the door. "See you tomorrow morning."

Tally marched over to Marc. "You're not going to let Mr. Johnson get away with destroying your peace march, are you?"

"It hardly seems worth having now. One hour and one sign and barely a dozen people isn't going to make much impression."

"He's infringing on your constitutional right of free speech."

"It doesn't seem fair for him to pay more attention to some crazy letters than to the rights of his students to express themselves on an important subject."

"He's more interested in protecting his job than he is in student rights."

"I don't see what we can do, though, except follow his orders."

"Suppose he should decide tomorrow morning to make you call off the whole thing. Would you just give in to him?"

"If I didn't, I'd get expelled."

"Which is more important, staying in this prison where you're being brainwashed by the establishment or standing up for your rights as an individual?"

Marc shook his head. "I don't know, Tally. You've got me all confused. Everything was so simple when I first started organizing this demonstration, but suddenly it's gotten so complicated."

"That's the fault of the establishment. They like to get things all muddied up so people lose their sense of what's right and wrong. It's another way of protecting their interests."

Marc shrugged into his overcoat and pulled his hat out of the pocket. Tally jumped in front of him, blocking his way to the door. "You aren't going home, are you?"

"There's no reason to hang around, is there?"

"Aren't you going back and tell Mr. Johnson we refuse to accept his restrictions on our march?"

Marc stared at her. "Of course not."

"You're going to give in without a fight?" She put both hands against his chest and pushed him against the blackboard.

"Tally, this is supposed to be a peace demonstration."

"And I thought you had the makings of a good revolutionary. You don't even know what the word means." She turned on her heel and ran out the door and down the corridor.

# Chapter Nine

**H**EY, LOOK, everyone's out on the grass," Marc said as the small red car labored up the high school driveway the next morning.

"Maybe one of the boilers blew up," Steve said. "Shall I let you off before I go park?"

Marc hopped out of the slowly moving car as it passed the flagpole. Helen and Nancy rushed up to him. "Marc, guess what?"

"There's been a bomb scare."

"Yeah," said John, "someone phoned up Mr. Johnson about twenty minutes ago and told him two bombs had been planted in the school."

"It's to teach him not to allow communists to use town property to spread their propaganda on."

"Yeah, this bomb threat guy said your march was

a desecration of the flag and of all that our country stands for."

Marc stood in the center of the group glancing from one to the other with a bewildered look on his face. "I don't understand it," he said in a choked voice to Helen. "Why has the idea of demonstrating for peace gotten everyone so stirred up?"

"There's a reporter around, too, Marc." John pointed to a man in a raincoat talking to a group of students on the sidewalk. "He's from one of the city papers. He said someone phoned in a tip that there was going to be some excitement up here this morning. He said he wanted to talk to you when you got here."

"Here he is." Helen stepped back and the reporter edged up to Marc.

"Hello there, Marc. I understand you're the organizer of this peace protest."

Marc nodded.

"And your demonstration is connected with the worldwide one this Mobilization for Peace group has organized for today?"

Marc nodded again.

"Any idea who might have phoned in the bomb threats or written those letters to your principal?"

Marc shook his head.

"Mind if I take your picture?"

"I wish you wouldn't."

Before Marc could turn his back, the reporter had raised the little camera hanging around his neck and snapped his picture, full face and close up. "Now where's that girl Tally Dayton some of the students told me was part of your group?"

"Here I am." Tally shouldered between Helen and Nancy.

"Tally, what have you done to your cape?" Helen screamed.

Tally spread out her cape and whirled around. Sewn on the back in big white ragged cloth letters were the words *Make love, not war.* "Isn't it cool? It's our sign."

"But it doesn't just say *Peace* like Mr. Johnson said it should."

"Hold it, Tally. I want a picture of that." The reporter focused his camera on the cape, and rapidly clicked and wound it several times.

"That's why I'm late. It took me longer than I expected to sew on the letters." Tally looked at the students milling around on the sidewalks, the grass, and the driveways. "What's going on?"

"Somebody phoned in a bomb threat. We're waiting for the firemen to get through searching the buildings for the bombs."

"How do they do that? Open every door of every locker and closet and all the drawers and everything? It will take them forever. We'll freeze before they're through."

"They have a thing which can smell explosives," a boy said. "It won't take them very long."

Tally turned to Marc. "Has Mr. Johnson said anything about whether we can still have the demonstration?"

"Not yet."

"Here come the firemen."

"Guess they didn't find anything."

A boy snapped his fingers disappointedly. "I was hoping they'd find a bomb just too late so we could all go home."

"Hey, the PA system is on. Someone's going to make an announcement." From the loudspeaker mounted on the corner of the cafeteria came the sound of breathing, then a muttered aside. Then Mr. Johnson cleared his throat and spoke.

"Students, in view of the bomb threat made this morning and the letters which I received on Monday and Tuesday from citizens who are opposed to the proposed peace demonstration at the flagpole today I have decided that the proposed demonstration must be canceled. The buildings have all been declared safe by the fire department so all students will please go to their first-period classes."

"Guess that's that," John said.

Tally held out her arms. "You aren't going in, are you?"

"You heard what he said." Helen ducked under Tally's arm and followed Nancy across the grassy circle around the flagpole and up the sidewalk toward the school.

"Fine bunch of fair-weather idealists," Tally sputtered.

Marc hunched against the flagpole with his arms folded over his stomach and stared at the ground. Slowly the crowd of students ebbed into the build-

106

ings. In a few minutes he and Tally were the only ones left outside.

"You kids going to stick it out?"

Marc looked up. The reporter clicked his camera twice more in rapid succession, raised the fingers of his right hand in the peace sign, and hurried toward a small battered car parked across the road from the flagpole. Tally folded her arms which were wrapped up in her cape and stared down at him, smiling. Marc sighed wearily and stood up.

"Well. I guess there isn't anything left to do except march."

"Right. While we have the chance." Tally hooked her arm through his, letting her cape fly out behind. "Too bad you don't have some kind of a sign, too."

"It doesn't matter. After all that excitement everyone must know what we're out here for."

Tally shook his arm. "Aren't you glad? Now, instead of just a few people getting your message the whole school has gotten it."

"I imagine they're thinking more about the bomb scare than they are about peace." Marc continued trudging around the flagpole, his hands in his pockets and his eyes on the ground. Overhead the halyards rattled against the pole and the flag streamed out flapping and snapping in the wind. Tally leaned against the pole, her cape wrapped around her, and stared angrily at the school.

"Why doesn't something happen? You don't suppose he's just going to leave us out here to freeze, do you?"

"I don't know." Marc raised his eyes as he passed her, and dropped them again.

Tally tipped back her head. "Maybe we should haul the flag down and burn it or tear it up or wear it or something."

"You leave the flag alone. We're in enough trouble already."

"Do you suppose he's going to call the police? I hope he does."

Marc stopped marching and stared at her. "Why?"

"Then everyone will see what a repressive reactionary fascist he is."

Marc kicked the cement flagpole pedestal angrily. "Will you cut out that kind of talk?"

"Oh, all right." Tally paced back and forth in front of the flagpole. "Maybe I should throw a rock through the cafeteria window. That would bring some action."

"You'd better not. Here comes a police car."

"Great." Tally hooked her arm through Marc's again. "Remember, if they start to beat you up, crouch down and cover up your head with your arms. And when they try to drag you over to the police car go absolutely limp and dead-weight."

The blue car slowed at the top of the hill. The man inside stared at them, then picked up his two-way radio and talked into it as the car circled the flagpole. The second time around the car stopped and the policeman rolled down his window.

"I thought Mr. Johnson said there wasn't going to be a protest march up here."

"I guess you thought wrong." Tally stuck out her chin and stared pugnaciously at the policeman.

"You kids better get back in your classes and tend to business."

"You going to try and make us?" Tally advanced on the police car with her fists clenched.

Marc pulled her back. "What are you trying to do, make him mad?"

"Of course I am, you stupid."

"Well, quit it. This is a peace demonstration and it's going to stay peaceful. Otherwise, what's the point in it?"

The policeman looked at them curiously. "You kids wouldn't have any idea who phoned in the bomb threats, would you?"

"Was there more than one?" Marc asked.

"The church was threatened, too."

"Do you have any idea?" Tally asked.

"We're working on it. Now why don't you kids beat it back into school?"

"Don't you give me orders," Tally cried.

The policeman shrugged, rolled up his window, and drove away. "Pig," Tally yelled after the car.

"Tally, he's a nice guy," Marc protested.

"No policeman's a nice guy." Tally watched the blue car disappear down the hill, then sat down on the pedestal again, and dropped her chin on her hands. "Maybe we should march into the office and confront Mr. Johnson there."

"Look, for the last time. We're out here to protest for peace. Now, are you going to march with me while we have the chance, or aren't you?"

Tally got up slowly and took his arm again. "This is the most boring protest I've ever been in."

"You asked to join it."

Tally looked over her shoulder. "Oh, wow, here comes Mr. Johnson at last. Now maybe we'll get some action."

The principal hurried down the sidewalk and across the road to the flagpole, his head lowered and his suit coat collar turned up against the wind. Tally clasped her cape around her and looked at him defiantly. "Don't you dare touch us. We have a right to express our opinions."

"I'm not going to. I came out to ask you two to please come into my office. I want to have a talk with you."

"Suppose we refuse to go?"

Mr. Johnson shook his head. "I have no obligation to you, Tally, except that of one human being to another. The only reason I let you enroll in this school is because Miss Tracey came and asked me to please let you come and promised she would be responsible for you. She's the one you put on the spot if you don't come in, not me."

"What'll you do if I don't come?"

"I shall expel you. Permanently."

"Expel me for insisting on my constitutional right of free speech?"

"It's too cold to stand out here and argue with

111

you. Come into the office and talk or leave. But if you leave you are never to come on the school property again."

"Marc, are you going with him? Aren't you going to stand up for your rights?" Without answering, Marc trudged across the road and up the sidewalk toward the building which held the principal's office. Mr. Johnson looked at Tally.

"Miss Tracey's in the office."

"So what? I'm not going with you."

Mr. Johnson turned on his heel and hurried after Marc. When he had almost reached the door Tally cupped her hands around her mouth. "Pig," she shouted at the top of her lungs. "Pig, pig, pig. You're all pigs."

# Chapter Ten

WHEN MARC APPEARED in the doorway of Mr. Johnson's office, Miss Tracey and the chief of police were sitting there quietly. They both looked up and the chief pointed to a battered, heavy yellow oak straight chair in front of the window. Marc tiptoed over to it, took off his overcoat, dropped it on the floor, and sat down on the edge of the chair.

"Principal coming?" the chief asked.

Marc nodded.

"Where's Tally?" Miss Tracey pushed back one wing of her long hair and looked anxiously at him. "She's coming, isn't she?"

Marc shook his head.

"I'd better go out and talk to her." As Miss Tracey

started to get up Mr. Johnson came into the room, turning down his coat collar and smoothing down his straight, iron-gray hair.

"No, stay right here, Wendy. She has to make the decision by herself whether to go or stay."

Mr. Johnson sat down and gestured toward the chief of police. "I guess the floor's yours, Tom."

The chief turned to Marc. "You know making bomb threats is against the law, don't you?"

"Why are you telling me? I didn't make them."

"Do you know who did?"

"No."

The chief frowned warningly. "Look, if you lie you'll just make things worse for yourself."

"But I don't know who did it."

"You had no knowledge that the threats were going to be made?"

"No."

"How about those letters to Mr. Johnson? Do you know who wrote those?"

Marc shook his head.

"This peace demonstration was your idea?"

Marc pulled the worn and folded letter from the Mobilization for Peace committee out of his jeans pocket and handed it to the chief. "I was just following their suggestion. It seemed like a good idea. I never dreamed it would stir up so much trouble."

The chief unfolded the letter and glanced at it quickly. "This committee didn't send you any separate instructions about using tactics like threatening letters and bomb threats to cause disruption in the

school and bring about a confrontation with the authorities?"

"That was the only letter I got. I met one of the guys whose name is on the letterhead at a peace rally I went to on the Common last summer and I guess he remembered my name and sent me the letter about today's demonstrations, thinking I might be interested in doing something about it."

The chief handed the letter back to Marc. "You should be careful these days what organizations you get connected with. A lot of them are fronts for groups with some pretty violent ideas, you know."

Marc nodded and stuffed the letter back into his jeans.

"The person who wrote the letters and made the bomb threat calls was one of your club members. You sure you don't know who it was?"

"One of the Foreign Affairs club members?" Marc stared at the chief with his mouth open.

"Don't call me a member of that stupid little organization. I never saw such a bunch of timid, middle-class reactionaries in my life." Tally stalked into the office, threw her wadded-up cape on the floor, and perched on the windowsill close to Marc's chair.

Marc twisted around and looked up at her. "Did you send the letters and make the bomb threat calls?"

"You sure are naive. I kept waiting for you to catch on and say something but you never did."

"But why? You spoiled everything."

"I couldn't believe you were serious about your

demonstration really being just for peace. The cause of every demonstration I've ever been mixed up with has just been an excuse to bring on a showdown with the establishment. I was sure you were doing the same thing."

"But I told you when we went for that walk the other night that it was strictly a peace demonstration. Why didn't you leave things alone?"

Tally swung her right leg, banging her boot heel against the wall. "I thought you'd all be grateful for a little excitement."

"Do your parents know where you are?" the police chief asked her.

"If you're thinking of sending me home, you're wasting your time. They don't want me."

"Have they made any attempt to find you since you ran away?"

"No."

"How do you know?"

"I've been gone nearly four months and I'm still out loose, aren't I? If they were looking for me I'd have been picked up by now or the police in this country are even dumber than I think they are."

"Or else you're pretty good at hiding."

Tally slipped off the windowsill and leaned on the back of Marc's chair. "Listen. I'll tell you why I know they aren't looking for me. The day before I left home I was having an argument with my father."

"About what?" the chief asked.

Tally waved her hand impatiently. "I don't remember now for sure, we had so many. I think it was about some of my friends he didn't like. I told him if he didn't stop trying to order me around and run my life as if I was still two years old, I'd run away."

She paused. The others were quiet, watching her. She closed her eyes for a minute and swallowed. "You know what he said? He said, 'Go ahead, see if I care. You've been nothing but trouble since you were ten years old.'"

"Oh, Tally," Miss Tracey murmured.

"And you know what else he said?" Tally took a few steps toward the police chief. "He said, 'And if you run away you needn't think I'll send the police out to find you. You leave this house without my permission and you don't ever need to come back.' That's what he said. I haven't forgotten a single word."

Miss Tracey jumped up and threw her arms about Tally. For a moment Tally let her head rest on the teacher's shoulder, then she straightened and pushed her away. "I don't care. I can take care of myself and I like being free to do just what I want." She stalked back to the windowsill and perched on it again.

"You aren't going to arrest her for making those bomb threats, are you?" Miss Tracey asked the police chief. Before he could answer Tally interrupted.

"How did you find out I made those phone calls?"

"You were seen in the pay phone booth across the

street from Avery's about the time the bomb threats were made."

"So?"

The chief smiled. "Talking with a handkerchief over your mouth."

Tally wrinkled her forehead and stared at the opposite wall. "Who was standing outside of Avery's then?" She punched Marc on the shoulder. "It was your sister and some other kids fooling around while they waited for Nancy and Jerry to come along and pick them up." She turned to the chief. "Wasn't it Sharon Ainsworth who told you?"

He nodded. She punched Marc again. "Your sister. She was the one who spread all the gossip about me the first day I was here in school. I always knew she hated me. Now I suppose you'll hate me, too."

"No, I don't hate you. I try not to hate anyone."

Tally leaned back against the window and folded her arms. "I wish I could say the same."

The police chief stood up, holding his cap in his hand. "I think this is a problem for the school, Bill, not for the police. I'll leave it up to you to decide how you want to deal with it."

When he had gone Mr. Johnson leaned forward and laid two white envelopes on the corner of his desk nearest Marc and Tally. "These are your suspension notices. Tally, I want you to stay out until the beginning of next week. Marc, you can come back as soon as you report to me accompanied by both your parents."

"Suppose I just up and leave town," Tally said, "and never come back to school at all on Monday morning?"

"That's up to you," Mr. Johnson said.

Miss Tracey held out her hand. "Don't go, Tally."

"I'll think about it." She picked up her cape, shook it out, and put it on inside out to hide the ragged cloth letters. "Can we go now?"

Mr. Johnson nodded. Marc put on his overcoat and pulled his cap down over his forehead. "You have your key?" Miss Tracey asked Tally. She nodded.

"That wasn't so bad," she said as she and Marc walked down the hill toward town. "When I saw the police chief there, I thought sure we were going to end up in jail."

Marc looked at the white envelope in his hand and stuffed it into his coat pocket. "It's all over for you, but I still have to face my father."

"Don't go home."

Marc stared at her. "What do you mean?"

"Run away," she said impatiently. "Go up to your family's cottage and hide out for a while."

"I couldn't do that."

"Why not? Are you scared?"

He shook his head and tried to smile jokingly. "The food's too good at home."

She laughed. "Well, that's something. You never knew at our house how it was going to be. Depended on Mother's mood. And how much she'd had to drink during the day."

120

They stood for a moment on the corner across from Avery's. "You going to walk all the way home?" Tally asked.

"Maybe someone I know will pick me up."

"You going to go back to school tomorrow with your parents?"

"I suppose so. I don't think Dad will want me to miss any classes."

"Well, maybe I'll see you again and maybe I won't. Depends on if I decide to stick around this place or move on."

"Yeah? Well, so long."

Tally grabbed Marc's coat sleeve as he was about to cross the street. "You aren't mad at me for getting you into this mess, are you?"

"I told you, no. I'm not mad."

"I wish there were more people like you." She let go of his sleeve and raised her hand. "Good-bye."

"Bye." He looked both ways, tucked his head down into his collar, and strode across the street.

"Marc! Marc!" He turned around and looked back. Tally was still standing on the opposite corner. She cupped her hands around her mouth. "I'm sorry."

He pulled one hand out of his pocket and waved, then huddled down inside his overcoat, and trudged toward home with his eyes on the ground. The wind was cold and an occasional snowflake whirled through the air. No one offered him a ride, but he didn't mind. He was in no hurry to get home.

When he finally arrived, he found Budge's car

sitting in the driveway. His fingers closed nervously over the white envelope in his pocket. As he passed the car on his way to the kitchen door he saw that the windshield had been hit with something and was a mass of cracks. There was a deep dent on the hood and several smaller ones on the fenders.

Budge was talking on the telephone when he opened the door and eased into the kitchen. Jean was sitting at the kitchen table. When she saw Marc she put her finger to her lips. Marc took off his coat, dropped it on the floor, and sat down across from his mother.

"What happened to the car?" he whispered.

Jean shook her head, then nodded toward Budge who was pacing back and forth with the telephone in one hand and a drink in the other.

"That's right," Budge said. "It happened in the company parking lot. Just as I got into my car and started the engine the windshield was shattered, and as I drove out a lot more rocks were thrown at me and my hood and fenders got dented."

He swallowed a large gulp from his glass while the person on the other end of the line spoke. His face flushed. "Well, my policy had better cover it. What have I been paying for all these years?"

He took another gulp and nodded impatiently. "I'm not interested in your opinion, Miss Borwin. You send me those forms right away. If I have to, I'll take my case all the way to the president of your company. Someone's going to pay for the repairs to my car and it isn't going to be me."

He hung up, swallowed the last of his drink, and set the glass down hard on the counter. "Stupid woman. She's not sure they insure me against vandalism or rioting."

He opened the freezer compartment of the refrigerator, took a handful of ice cubes out of the storage container, rattled them into his glass, and splashed some whiskey over them from the open bottle on the shelf. "Hello, Marc, what are you doing home? I thought school didn't let out until two."

"I got let out early." Marc hauled his coat up on his lap and pulled out the envelope. "I got suspended."

# Chapter Eleven

S<small>USPENDED</small>? W<small>HY</small>?" Budge tore open the envelope and looked at the notice inside.

Marc slipped lower in his chair. "The peace march," he muttered.

"You went ahead with that after I expressly forbade you to have anything to do with it?"

Marc nodded miserably.

Budge pointed to the kitchen window that looked out on the driveway. "Did you see my car? Do you know how it got that way?"

Marc shook his head.

"Your Mobilization for Peace Day demonstrators did that. If they're for peace I prefer war any day."

"What made them so angry, dear?" Jean asked.

"They seemed to think it was a personal insult that

we announced our acquisition of Brown Chemical Company today."

Marc sat up. "The company that makes nerve gas and herbicides and napalm for the government?"

"And insecticides for farmers and rat poison and a few other useful products," Budge said sarcastically. "Yes, that's the company I mean. United Products has bought a controlling interest in it."

"But why did these demonstrators throw rocks at your car, dear? You weren't responsible for the company's buying Brown Chemical."

"I just happened to be the first car out of the gate after the president closed the company at noon because those peaceniks were getting so violent. They were refusing to let salesmen into the office and turning away the delivery trucks and blocking the sidewalks and the road in front of the building."

"Did anyone from United Products make an effort to hear their point of view?" Marc asked.

"Of course we did. The president asked them to send in some representatives to talk the situation over. What a waste of effort. He'd have done better to have called the police and had the whole crowd dispersed right then instead of waiting till later when they really got out of hand."

Budge sloshed the ice and liquid around in his glass. "It was unbelievable. If those people are going to be the leaders of the next generation, this country is ruined. They sent in four people, a girl and three men. Most unattractive people I've ever seen. Couldn't tell the girl from the boys, or maybe it was

125

the other way around. Between the hair and the beards there was enough natural material for two dozen wigs. Not one of them had on a proper pair of shoes or a decent article of clothing and yet they were all college students. I don't know what kind of people we're educating these days."

"What did you all talk about?" Marc asked.

"We didn't talk. The president asked what they wanted. They handed him a piece of paper with their demands written on it. Not only did they want us to give up all our government contracts immediately, but they wanted us to announce publicly, right then, that U.P. would give up its ownership of Brown Chemical." Budge snorted. "That was all."

"What did the president say?"

Budge stared at Marc over his glass. "What do you think he said? He said no, only he said it in a more polite and roundabout way than that. He told them that we had considered the fact that a percentage of Brown Chemical's sales was to the government but that we were hoping to lower that percentage, that a majority of our stockholders had been in favor of the acquisition, and that we had committed a lot of money to the acquisition and it would be impossible for us to give it up now."

"What did he say about the government contracts U.P. has now?"

"He told them politely but firmly to mind their own business and leave United Products to mind its. Then he had them shown out."

126

"I suppose they didn't like that very much," Jean said.

"They certainly didn't. The crowd got bigger and bigger and noisier and noisier so finally the president decided to close down for the rest of the day."

"I'm so glad you didn't get hurt, dear." Jean came over and hugged Budge as he stood looking out the window at his car.

"It's a good thing that little car has plenty of power. Some of those hoodlums tried to jump me as I came out the gate. I don't know what they were trying to do, but I didn't wait around to find out."

Budge finished his drink, slammed down his glass, and spun around toward Marc. "Okay, now explain to me why you got suspended. Did you set fire to the building or break all the windows or burn up the records to show how much you love peace?"

"There was a bomb scare."

"Speak up. I can't hear when you mumble. A bomb scare? Were you responsible for it?"

Marc shook his head.

"Who was?"

"Tally."

"I knew that girl was trouble the minute I saw her. How do you feel now about her wonderful ideas?"

"She's kind of radical, I admit, but it's not her fault. Her mother's an alcoholic and her father doesn't understand her at all."

"That's right. Blame everything on the parents.

127

When are you kids going to realize that you've got to be responsible for your own actions?"

"Well, if a man has a child I don't think he has any right to tell her that if she runs away he doesn't ever want her to come back."

"Oh, no," Jean exclaimed. "What a dreadful thing to do."

"If any child of mine was ungrateful enough for all that I've done for him to run away I'd tell him exactly the same thing."

"Well, I wouldn't," Jean said defiantly. "My children will always be welcome in this house no matter what they've done."

"Let's not argue about it now." Budge took a few impatient steps up and down in front of Marc. "So what happened after the bomb scare?"

"Mr. Johnson said we couldn't march at all."

"He'd given you permission previously to march?"

"For an hour, with one sign and only a few people."

"So you marched anyway, in spite of his ordering you not to?"

Marc nodded.

"And that girl marched, too, I suppose."

"Yes."

Budge leaned against the counter and stared at Marc's bowed head, his lips pressed angrily together. The sound of the front door banging open and slamming shut sounded extra-loud in the oppressive silence of the kitchen.

Jean jumped. "Is that you, Sharon?"

"Daddy, what happened to your car?" Sharon hurried into the kitchen and dropped her armful of books on the telephone stool.

"I was caught in a peace demonstration." Budge turned again to glower down at Marc.

"That's what I thought." Sharon flapped open the newspaper she was carrying. "It tells about it here. And about the one we had at school, too. Did you hear about the bomb scare?"

"Yes, I heard about the bomb scare."

Sharon tapped on the paper. "See, there's Marc's picture and that girl's and all of us standing around outside while the firemen looked for bombs. It was very exciting."

Budge snatched the paper. Jean crept up close and looked over his shoulder. "What does it say on that girl's cape?"

"*Make love, not war.* Isn't that wild?" Sharon giggled. "She cut the letters out of an old sheet."

"That's a terrible picture of Marc," Jean said. "It makes him look like those awful people you see in Harvard Square."

"Let's face it, Mother, that's how he does look." Sharon took an apple out of the bowl on the shelf and bit into it noisily.

Budge's eyes flicked rapidly over the columns of newsprint and then rested once more on the close-up picture of Marc with his name printed underneath it in small black letters. Convulsively he folded the paper together and slapped his palm with it.

"You realize, young man, that you've probably

ruined my chances of any more promotions at United Products with this day's escapade?"

Marc looked up. "I'm sorry, Dad."

"A lot of good that's going to do. Jean, where are the clippers you used to cut Marc's hair with when he was little?"

"They're upstairs, dear."

"Get them."

"What are you going to do?"

Budge threw the newspaper across the room. "I'm going to cut Marc's hair. I've been very patient up to now with him, but today is the last straw. There's nothing can undo the damage he's already done but if he doesn't look like a hippie anymore maybe he'll stop acting like one and I can have some peace."

"Dad, I'm not a hippie."

"That reporter calls you one in that article." He stamped across the room, picked up the paper, and opened it up with a snap. " 'Leaders of the peace demonstration were Marc Ainsworth, the most color-ful-appearing student in the school in the opinion of his fellow students, and Tally Dayton, former member of the hippie subcultures of New York and Boston, now living in Warton with a member of the social studies department, Miss Gwendolyn Tracey.' "

"He doesn't come right out and say I'm a hippie."

"This picture of you dispels any doubt that remains."

"My hair isn't doing anyone any harm, Dad."

"You got yourself suspended today, didn't you?"

"But not because of my hair."

Budge slapped the newspaper down on the counter. "It's all part of the same thing. I'm not going up to that school with you to get you reentered until your hair is cut and neither is your mother."

"Then I won't go back to school. I'll get a job."

Budge jerked him to his feet and shook him. "You will not. Jean, where are those clippers?" He looked over his shoulder toward the hall and yelled again for his wife.

Jean ran into the kitchen with a box in her hands. "I'm sorry, dear, I couldn't find them at first. It's been so long since anyone's used them."

"Plug them in." Budge took Marc by the back of the neck, hauled him closer to the counter, picked up the clippers, and snapped them on.

Marc twisted his head to look up at his father. "Please, Dad, don't do it."

"Hold still."

"Mom, make him stop."

"Budge, do you think you should?"

"Shut up, both of you." Budge pulled a large lock of hair away from Marc's temple and attacked it at the roots with the clippers.

Marc winced.

"Budge, you're hurting him."

"If you don't want to watch you can leave the room." Budge grabbed another hunk of hair and chewed at it with the clippers.

"Oh, Daddy," Sharon whispered nervously. "He's going to look so funny."

Jean dropped into her chair and watched with her

knuckles jammed against her mouth as hunk after hunk of long, pale brown hair fell to the floor. When he was through Budge snapped off the clippers, dropped them on the counter, and brushed some long strands of hair off the backs of his hands.

"Clean up that mess," he ordered Marc. "And when you're through go to your room and stay there until your mother calls you for supper." He picked up his glass, grabbed the bottle off the shelf, and strode down the hall to his study.

Marc stood motionless, his eyes on the floor. "Oh, my baby." Jean threw her arms around him and tried to draw his head on to her shoulder.

"Don't, Mom." He pushed her away with the point of his shoulder, and picked a strand of hair off his sleeve. Jean brushed off his back.

"You go upstairs, dear. I'll clean up."

Marc shuffled out of the kitchen, dragging his overcoat behind him. Upstairs in his room he dropped face down on his bed and gently touched the ragged tufty ends of his hair with his finger tips.

After a while he rolled over and stared at the ceiling, then pushed himself off the bed, turned on the light in his closet, and stood for a long time in front of the mirror on his closet door. Then he nodded firmly as if he had made a decision, pulled his knapsack off his closet shelf, set it on the floor, and began to drop things in it from the drawers which he quietly pulled open and neglected to close. When the knapsack was full, he pulled the drawstring up tight,

buckled down the flap, and carried it over to the other side of the room.

Then he hung up his overcoat after taking his woolen hat out of the pocket and putting it on, kicked off his ragged sneakers and put on his heavy hiking boots, put on a heavy sweater and a parka, took some money out of his desk drawer, and turned out the closet light.

Quietly he eased open the front window nearest the corner of his room and looked out. The street lights were on but the street was deserted. Below him a patch of light shone on the brown grass from the lamp which someone had turned on in the living room. He tiptoed to the bedroom door, opened it a crack, and listened for a moment. From downstairs came the sounds of Jean getting dinner in the kitchen and the record player going loudly in the living room.

He frowned. Then the telephone rang and Sharon shouted, "Let me get it. It's probably for me." As she ran from the living room to the kitchen, Marc quickly shut his door, strode across the room, picked up his knapsack, and threw it out the open window. Then, leaning out, he grasped the downspout of the gutter pipe and shinnied to the ground.

Half an hour later when Jean opened his bedroom door, she was met by a blast of cold air from the still-open window of the empty room.

# Chapter Twelve

THE BUS DRIVER looked over his shoulder at Marc, sitting on the edge of the seat behind him. "Where'll I let you off?"

Marc peered through the thick cloud of snowflakes swirling past the bus window. "Do you go into the center of town?"

"Only as far as the post office. Then I turn off."

"Okay, I'll get off there." Marc put on his pack and stood up, clinging to the steel pole behind the driver as the bus chuffed down a long grade into the main street of a small town. After making a left turn the driver pulled over to the curb in front of the low, yellow-brick post office with the name CENTRE DANBY over the heavy plate glass doors. The bus door hissed open, Marc hopped out onto the sidewalk, and the bus pulled away.

Already the snow on the ground was several inches deep. Marc ducked his head and strode around the corner to the main street. The wind drove the snow into his face and down his neck. In the middle of the block, the lights of a supermarket gleamed faintly through the dull, gray morning light. He pushed open the door and went in, stamping the snow from his boots and brushing it off the front of his parka. The big, warm store was nearly empty. Two of the checkout clerks were leaning against their cash registers talking. Marc trundled a wagon slowly past them.

"Did you hear the latest weather report?" one of them said to the other.

"I heard one at six. Said we were going to get at least a foot."

"The one I heard on my car radio on the way to work said a foot and a half with high winds and lots of drifting."

The other one looked out the window. "I hope we close early. Last time we had a big storm I had to spend the night at my sister's and her kid kept me awake all night with his crying."

For a long time Marc wandered up and down the aisles, putting items into his basket and then quite often retracing his steps and putting them back on the shelves. When he at last pushed his cart up to the checkout counter, he had in it a small bag of potatoes, a carton of dried milk, a small canned ham, and a bag of oranges.

The clerk looked at him curiously as he dropped his purchases on the conveyor belt. Briskly she punched the cash register keys while he pushed the wagon back to the others by the front door. "That's six dollars and six cents. You staying in some camp around here?"

Marc nodded as he pulled his billfold out of his pants pocket.

"You didn't pick a very good day to come. Was it snowing where you came from?"

"A little." Marc counted out the exact change and handed it to her.

"You can't be going to stay long if that's all you're buying to eat." She put the money in the drawer, slammed it shut, and pulled a brown paper bag out from under the counter.

Marc smiled.

"Talkative guy, aren't you?"

"I bet he's a hippie going up to visit those people at the old Danby farm," the other clerk said as Marc tramped to the door.

He set off down the street, his arms wrapped around his bag. After another block of stores, the business section of Centre Danby ended, and old-fashioned houses set back under large, bare trees lined both sides of the street. Gently the road began to go uphill. The sidewalk ended. The houses thinned out and the farms began.

Snow began to pile up on top of the brown bag,

137

on his shoulders and his pack. He pulled the hood of his parka farther forward and ducked his chin deeper into the turtleneck of his sweater. Suddenly a pickup truck going the other way rattled past, its lights shining feebly through the thick snow. There was no other sign of life. Not even a dog barked as he trudged by a yellow farmhouse.

At the top of the long rise he stopped for a moment and looked around. He knew that at the bottom of the long, sloping expanse of open pasture on his left was the lake, but it was invisible through the snow. Also invisible were the wooded hills which encircled the lake. He took a fresh grip on his groceries and trudged on. After a while he heard behind him the muffled throbbing of another vehicle. He moved over to the shoulder. In a moment the same blue pickup truck which had gone the other way not long before passed him. A few yards down the road it squeaked to a halt and backed up. The door on the passenger side was flung open and a small, dark man with a red knitted cap perched on the back of his head leaned out.

"Hey, mon gars, you want a ride?"

"Sure. You got room?" Marc peered into the cab.

The small dark man squeezed over close to the driver, a big man with a copper-colored beard and mustache. "Sure, we got room. How far you go?"

"A mile or so down the road, to the Ainsworth place."

The driver looked over at him with his eyes narrowed. "That place is all closed up."

"I know. It belongs to my family. I'm Marc Ainsworth." Marc scrambled into the cab and sat on the edge of the seat, his bag on his lap and his pack bumping up against the seat back.

"That so? I met Julius Ainsworth this summer. Is he your father?"

"No, my uncle."

"I'm Dan Ross and this is Louis Bastide. We live on the old Danby farm."

Marc nodded.

Louis crossed his arms and let his chin rest on his chest. "This is one lousy day, eh?"

Dan glanced at Marc who was peering out the window at the mailboxes along the side of the road. "The road to your cottage doesn't get plowed, you know. By tomorrow you're going to be snowed in."

"That's all right. I'm not planning to go anywhere."

"You're welcome to come and stay with us."

"Thanks, but I'd sort of like to be by myself for a while." Marc put his hand on the door handle as the truck's headlights picked up a mailbox with AINSWORTH painted on it in large black capital letters.

Dan stopped the truck. Marc climbed out and thanked him for the ride. The two men waved and the truck disappeared in the snow. Marc trudged briskly down the narrow winding unpaved road. Except for the hiss of the snow showering steadily down, the woods were absolutely still. The yellow clapboard cottage perched on the bank above the lakeshore was closed up tight with shutters on the windows of both stories and solid wooden panels screwed over the doors. He put his bag and his pack on the front porch and walked around the house several times wondering how to get in. Then he clumped down the wooden steps to the boathouse. His face brightened as he saw that the long wooden ladder which was there in the summer was still hanging on the back wall under the wide eaves. He dragged it back up to the cottage and propped it against the back wall under a small, square window, the only one left unshuttered.

The window was hooked on the inside. He balled his mittened fist, broke the pane, and undid the hook. The window swung open and he squeezed through it into the bathroom. The house was cold and musty-smelling. He clumped down the stairs and into the living room, pushed up the sash of one of the front windows, unhooked the shutter, and climbed out onto the front porch. After dropping his pack and bag over the windowsill into the living room, he took the ladder back to the boathouse, then stood for a minute on the shore and looked out at the snow blowing in thick gray curtains across the frozen, empty lake.

"Wow," he murmured, "this is nice."

All afternoon he worked to make himself comfortable. By the time darkness fell he was well settled in the square living room. A fire crackled in the airtight stove and a large pile of firewood from the cottage cellar was stacked nearby. Pans full of snow

140

were ranged around the stove on the floor and as fast as the snow turned to water he poured it into a large bucket and stepped out through the window to scoop up more. From a bedroom he dragged down a mattress and pillow and all the blankets which were in a chest in a closet. From the kitchen he brought in some crockery and utensils, a box of tea bags, a round carton of salt, and a jar of instant coffee.

"Sure didn't leave much food around when they closed up," he murmured as he put these things on the table with the food he had bought in Centre Danby.

As dusk fell, he made a last trip out the window to fill his pans once more with snow. Then he lighted the two kerosene lamps he had chosen from the row of lamps lined up on the kitchen shelf, hooked the shutter and closed the window, took off his parka, and set to work cooking his supper.

When he had finished eating, he stacked his dirty dishes on the table, dragged the mattress close to the stove, and began unfolding blankets. His watch said only a little after eight. He looked over the row of limp, well-worn paperback books in the bookcase between the two front windows, then shook his head.

"No, not tonight. It's been a long day and I sure didn't get much sleep last night in the bus station."

He turned out his lamps and climbed under the heap of blankets. Outside the wind whistled around the corner of the porch and flung the snow like sand against the side of the house. The glow from the stove gradually dimmed. By the time the ashes were cold, Marc had been asleep a long time.

When he woke up, the room was still dark although gray light showed through the cracks in the shutters. The blankets pulled up around his face were stiff where the moisture from his warm breath had frozen. Outside it sounded as if it was still snowing hard.

He crumpled up some newspaper, shoved it into the stove, threw in some kindling, and lit a match. Then he pulled the blankets around his shoulders and sat cross-legged on the mattress, every now and then laying a piece of wood on the fire until it was burning brightly and the room began to warm a little.

After eating an orange and drinking a cup of tea, he pulled on his boots without lacing them and shuffled across the floor to the window. It took several hard shoves to get the shutter open, and when he looked out he saw that during the night snow had drifted onto the porch and piled up so deeply that only the top of the railing showed. The trees were plastered with streaks of snow on their windward sides. The scrubby undergrowth was already buried, a thick blanket covered the boathouse roof, and it was still snowing hard.

"I might get snowed in at that," he said as he pulled down the window. "Guess I'd better stretch my supplies as much as I can."

He made himself another cup of tea, pulled a big

wicker armchair, which had corduroy-covered pads on the seat and back, up to the heat, and sprawled luxuriously with his stocking feet tucked under the stove. He yawned and his eyes closed. A sharp knocking on the glass of the unshuttered window awakened him. He sat up with a jerk and his cold tea slopped over his hands. He set the cup on the floor and looked around the wing of the chair. A man on snowshoes was bending down and looking in the window. Sleepily he pushed himself to his feet and padded over to open the window.

"You Marc Ainsworth?" the man asked.

Marc nodded.

"Albert Stourby. Maybe you don't remember me."

"Sure I do. How come you're out in weather like this?"

"Just checking to see how the porch is holding up under the weight of the snow. It has a rotten corner post. Mind if I come in for a minute?" Mr. Stourby unbuckled his snowshoes and managed to get them off, and himself in through the window, without sinking into the snow. He was a lean, wiry old man with a weatherbeaten face and bright blue eyes.

Marc put some more wood on the fire. "Would you like a cup of tea? I can get the water boiling in just a few minutes."

"That would be just the thing." Mr. Stourby took off his cap and mittens, unbuttoned his worn mackinaw jacket, and pulled a chair up close to the stove. As the fire grew hotter the smell of drying wool

filled the air. "You look mighty snug in here."

Marc looked around the room with satisfaction. "I am. The only thing I'm worried about is my food supply. It'll give out in a couple more days and I'm wondering if I can make it up to the road. How deep would you say the snow was?"

"Three feet anyway and more to come." Mr. Stourby took the cup Marc handed to him and jounced the tea bag up and down in the steaming water. "There used to be some snowshoes around here."

"They're in the basement but the mice have eaten the webbing."

"How long were you fixing to stay?"

"I haven't made up my mind."

"Folks know you're here?"

"I didn't tell them."

"You don't think they might be worried about your whereabouts?"

"I don't care. Let them worry."

The old man squeezed his tea bag dry with his fingers and threw it into the stove. "That's kind of an ungrateful way to talk."

Marc rubbed his palm over his cropped hair. "Look, Mr. Stourby, I don't want to be rude to you, but it's none of your business. My father did something to me that he shouldn't have done and the only thing left for me to do was leave home. I don't know when or if I'm ever going back. Now, let's forget it and talk about something else."

"You're mighty decided."

"I sure am."

Mr. Stourby drained his cup and stood up. "Guess I'd better be getting back. Mary'll start worrying I'm buried in a snowdrift and can't get out." At the window he turned around. "You got enough firewood?"

"There's a lot in the cellar."

"How's the kerosene supply?"

"There's a gallon can almost full."

"So you're all fixed except for food?"

"That's right."

When Mr. Stourby had gone, Marc scrubbed off a couple of potatoes, set them just inside the stove door to bake, then sat down to read. When the strong smell of charring potato skins filled the air, he opened the stove door and pulled the blackened lumps out onto a plate and added a slice of ham. He sniffed hungrily as he broke the potatoes open and sprinkled them with salt. Just as he was stuffing the first bite into his mouth he heard voices outside on the porch. He looked over his shoulder and saw the two men who had given him the ride the day before peering in the window. He set his plate down on his chair and went to let them in.

"Hey, mon gars." The little dark man climbed nimbly off his snowshoes and into the living room. "We came to see how you like this snowstorm."

Dan undid his snowshoes but in kicking them off he lost his balance and tumbled into the snow up to his hips. "Hey, Louis, give me a hand."

His friend grabbed him by the elbows and hauled

him in through the window, along with a cascade of snow. Dan looked down at the floor. "Almost as much inside as out. I'm sorry." He shut the window, then slapped at the snow which coated his heavy woolen pants.

"That's all right." Marc picked up his plate and sat down again. "Mind if I keep on eating my lunch while the potatoes are still hot?"

Louis sat down in the other chair and pulled off his red wool hat. "Oui, mon gars, you are très comfortable, n'est-ce pas? We needn't have worried about this one, eh, Dan? He's snug like the bug in the rug."

"Were you worried about me?" Marc looked up at Dan, standing next to the stove.

"A little."

Louis slapped his knee with his hat and laughed. "Not us, but les femmes. When we told them we had left you off to come down here all by yourself they made une grande clameur, n'est-ce pas, Dan? Le pauvre petit, il aura faim, il aura froid." Louis covered both ears with his hands and shook himself, laughing.

"That was very nice of them," Marc said. "But I can take care of myself." He opened the stove door and threw his orange peels into the fire, then dipped a pan full of water and set it on the stove to heat. "Guess it's time I did a few dishes. No sense getting everything in the place dirty."

"How long are you thinking of staying?" Dan asked.

"I don't know."

"Anything we can do for you?"

"I guess not, thanks."

"How about some snowshoes? We have an extra pair."

"That would be great. Then I could get up to the road and hitch a ride to town for groceries."

"You're not lonesome?" Louis asked.

Marc grinned. "I haven't been alone long enough yet."

Louis pulled on his cap and jumped up. "Allons, mon ami. Le garçon needs nothing and I must get back to my looms or ma femme, comme elle me grondera. Ma foi!" He scrambled out the window and somehow managed to get his snowshoes on without falling into the snow. Then he moved Dan's shoes up close to the windowsill and held out his hand. "Viens-tu, mon brave, and don't drown again in the snow. When you were a rich stockbroker in New York City you should have taken some ballet lessons."

"That's right," Dan wheezed as he crouched awkwardly on the windowsill. "You never know what you're going to need out in the country."

# Chapter Thirteen

By LATE AFTERNOON the snow had begun to taper
off, and by night the sky was clear. On a trip to
the cellar the next morning for firewood, Marc found
a rusty coal shovel leaning against the wall behind
the old furnace which had been converted to oil several years ago. He took it upstairs with him, and
when he had eaten an orange and drunk a cup of tea,
he dragged it out the window and began to clear the
snow off the porch.

The wind had dropped and the sun shone brightly.
Before long he took off his hat and laid it on the windowsill. A few minutes later he took off his parka and
finally his turtleneck sweater. He had cleared away
the snow from under his access window and was
making a wide path to the porch steps when he heard

voices. He plowed to the unshoveled end of the porch and looked up the road. His father and Mr. Stourby were snowshoeing down the road. He hurried back to the window and pulled on his hat, dragging it well down over his ears, then leaned on his shovel and waited for the two men to come around the corner of the porch.

His father saw him first. "Hello, Marc."

Marc nodded. Budge knelt at the bottom of the steps to unbuckle his snowshoes. Marc watched him unsmilingly.

"Maybe while you two talk I'll go have a look at the boathouse." Mr. Stourby hurried off on his snowshoes toward the lake.

Budge came slowly up the porch steps. "Been doing a little shoveling, I see."

"Yeah."

"Good for the figure."

"That's not why I'm doing it."

"No, no, of course not." Budge's face reddened. He took off the small pack he was wearing and held it out to Marc. "Some cookies and apples. Your mother sent them."

"Thanks." Marc set the pack on the windowsill without opening it. "How did you know where I was?"

"Tally said this is where you might have gone."

"Tally. How come you were talking to her?"

"I figured she was the one who put it into your head to run away, so I called her up as soon as we discovered you had gone."

Marc perched on the windowsill and crossed his arms. "That must have been quite a conversation."

"She wasn't very polite."

Marc looked at his father from under his eyebrows. "Were you?"

Budge unzipped his jacket with a jerk. "It was no time to be polite. Your mother was having hysterics and telling me it was all my fault and screaming at me to find you before something dreadful happened to you."

"I never told Tally where I was going. I just called her up from the pay phone to tell her I was leaving and say good-bye."

"That's what she said. I'm surprised she didn't want to come with you."

"I asked her."

"You did?"

"Sure."

"And she said no?"

"She said she was okay where she was for now and didn't plan to move on until spring."

"Like the gypsies."

"Oh, I don't think she'll run away again. She just said that to save face."

"Well, she certainly didn't make any effort to save mine. When I asked her if she had any ideas where you might have gone she said she did but she wasn't going to tell me since I didn't deserve to know. Then, after lecturing me for the next ten minutes on what a lousy father I was, she said, 'He's probably gone to your summer cottage,' and hung up."

"I'm surprised you didn't hang up on her first."

"I would have if it hadn't been for your mother."

"I'm sorry you had such a rough time."

Budge leaned up against the porch railing and stared off into the glittering woods. "It sure is peaceful up here."

Marc opened the little pack and pulled out a cookie. "What did you do after Tally told you I might be up here?"

"I tried to call Albert, but we couldn't get hold of him until the middle of yesterday morning because there was a bad connection somewhere so that we could hear him but he couldn't hear us."

"I thought it was kind of funny he should come snowshoeing down here in the middle of the storm just to see how the porch was holding up."

"He didn't want to do it but your mother cried so hard into the upstairs phone that he finally said he would."

"And so now you've come to take me home."

"You can't stay here."

"Why can't I?"

"Don't be ridiculous. You can't stay here all alone in a closed-up summer cottage just lying around doing nothing. You belong in school. And then think about your mother. She's in a terrible state over this affair."

"So what's new? She's in a state when I'm home, too."

"That's no way to talk. Your mother loves you in spite of the way you behave."

152

"My behavior wouldn't bother her if it didn't bother you."

"Are you or aren't you coming home?"

"No, I'm not. If I did the same old arguments would start all over again and we'd be worse off than before."

"Now listen here. I'm your father and you're going to do what I tell you."

Marc looked over at Budge and shook his head. "It won't work, Dad. I'm free now. If you want me to come home, you'll have to persuade me."

"All right, if that's the way you feel, stay. But don't expect to live under my roof again." Budge turned on his heel and stamped down the steps. As he was buckling on his second snowshoe Mr. Stourby clumped up the bank from the lakeshore.

"Budge, come with me a minute. A section of the boathouse roof is collapsing under the weight of the snow. I want to know what you want to do about it."

"I'm leaving." Budge glared up at Marc as he yanked on his harness strap.

"Well, before you do, come with me and have a look at this roof."

Budge pressed his lips together angrily and stamped down the bank behind Mr. Stourby. Marc went back to work shoveling the porch. The two men were out of sight for a long time but every so often Marc could hear his father's angry voice and then the murmur of Mr. Stourby's.

"How about boiling us up some tea, Marc?" Mr.

153

Stourby said when they finally reappeared. "Your dad's changed his mind about leaving right away."

Budge was the last to climb through the window into the living room. "Say, you've fixed yourself up pretty good. I couldn't have done better myself."

Marc turned around from stoking the fire and grinned. "I learned all I know from you. Remember those polar bear overnight camping trips with the Cub Scouts? Fixing myself up here was a snap compared to those."

"Yeah, they were pretty rigorous. Where can I find another chair?"

"In the kitchen." Marc dipped a pan of water out of the large bucket and put it on the stove to heat.

"How's Julius' new business coming along?" Mr. Stourby asked when they were finally all seated around the stove with their steaming teacups in their hands.

"He's doing fine," Budge said. "He's really cashing in on the big fuss over pollution with some process he has a patent for. I guess his company will get bigger before it gets smaller."

"That so? Maybe you and he should go into partnership. If your grandfather were alive he'd get a kick out of seeing another Ainsworth and Ainsworth doing business again."

"Oh, the company wouldn't be called that. Jules has already given it one of those fancy made-up names everyone is so fond of these days. Envirotronics."

"That's mighty impersonal. How's a body to know who he's doing business with?" Mr. Stourby reached down to the plate on the floor for another cookie.

"You look for the names of the corporate officers on the letterhead of the company stationery."

"Well, when the letterhead of Envirotronics has both your names on it, send me a piece."

"I'll do that."

Marc looked at his father eagerly. "Are you going to work for Uncle Julius?"

"I'm thinking of it. Things aren't as good at U.P. for me as they were. We just merged, you know, with a chemical company," Budge explained to Mr. Stourby, "and they've brought three of that company's men into our top management, which pretty well blocks me from going any higher."

"That's too bad. Never thought working for one of those big companies would be much fun, anyhow. Kind of a dog-eat-dog proposition, isn't it?"

"There's a lot of pressure," Budge admitted. "I won't mind getting away from that."

Marc sloshed the pan of water. "More tea, Dad?"

Budge held out his cup. "Pour it right over the old tea bag."

"Mr. Stourby?"

"No, thanks. I've got to be getting back."

After he had left, Budge sat on the edge of his chair, swirling his tea bag round and round in his cup. "Maybe you'd like me to go, too."

"No, Dad, I'm glad you stayed."

Budge swirled the tea bag some more. "You know, if I change jobs and go to work for Julius I'll probably have more time at home."

"That would be nice."

"You and I could maybe do some things together once in a while."

"Yeah, we could."

Budge looked up and smiled wryly. "I don't know what kind of things, though. You don't like golf and I don't go much for peace demonstrations."

"There's fishing. Remember when I was little and we'd go down to the river and fish off the bridge? Or take the canoe up to the bay? We never caught much, but it was fun."

"It was, wasn't it? Remember the time we tipped over?"

"And the time we stopped at the island and cooked the two bass we had caught? One mouthful for you and one for me, they were so small."

"You know, there used to be a lot of fishing tackle around this place. If I could find it, we could go ice fishing tomorrow. I'm going to take a look down cellar."

"You'll need a lamp."

"I'll get one in the kitchen."

Marc stacked the dirty cups on the table and had just picked up his book and sat down in the armchair to read when there was a sharp knock on the glass, the window was pushed up from outside, and Louis hopped into the room.

"Hello, mon petit. We've come to pay you a visit." He gave his hand to a woman as small and dark as he was and helped her through the window. "Here is my wife Phyllis, and Dan and his wife Nelda."

"We brought you a few things we thought might come in handy." Phyllis unslung a large, handwoven woolen bag from her shoulder and pulled out a loaf of bread, a large chunk of unsliced bacon, some eggs, a cabbage, a half-dozen large carrots, and a yellow turnip.

Marc took each thing from her as she pulled it out and put it on the table. "Wow, that's neat. We were all out of food. Did you bake the bread?"

"No, Nelda did."

"I don't know how good it is. Mr. Stourby keeps giving me helpful hints and every batch is an improvement over the last." Nelda Ross took off her long shapeless tweed coat and dropped it on the floor. She was a big woman with graying brown hair pulled back off her face in a thick braid which reached to her waist.

"We also brought you a pair of snowshoes," Dan said. "They're out on the porch."

"Hey, you folks are great. Why don't you all sit down? Would anyone like a cup of tea? It'll only take me a minute to boil the water."

Louis sat down in the big wicker armchair and pulled his wife down on his lap. "You see, ma chérie, you need not have worried about le garçon. Look how well he can manage."

Marc grinned as he put a full pan of water on the stove. "I'm getting awfully good at making tea." He went out into the kitchen for more clean cups and yelled down the cellar steps, "Hey, Dad, we've got company."

Budge came into the living room a few minutes later carrying a dusty gray tackle box. Marc finished pouring the water into the cups and set the pan back on the stove. "This is my dad, everybody. Dad, this is Mr. and Mrs. Ross and Mr. and Mrs. Bastide."

Louis pushed Phyllis off his lap and jumped up, his hand out. "Louis Bastide, m'sieur, my wife Phyllis, Dan and Nelda Ross." He turned on Marc. "What is this monsieur and madame stuff, eh?"

"Budge Ainsworth. How do you do?"

Budge set the tackle box on the floor and shook hands with everyone.

"Thinking of doing some fishing?" Dan asked.

"I thought I might. Show Marc here how it's done. I used to get some big ones through the ice when I was a boy."

"You're going to stay here for awhile?"

"Through tomorrow anyway."

Marc sat down on the floor. "Look over on the table, Dad. Now we have something besides apples and oranges to eat."

"Your own produce?" Budge asked Dan.

Dan nodded.

"Were you always a farmer?"

"Not him." Louis leaned forward, his arms clasped around Phyllis. "Eight months ago he was a rich stockbroker in New York City who didn't know the difference between a yellow turnip and a white one."

"And what were you?"

"Me, what was I?" Louis looked up at Phyllis.

She pulled his red hat down over his nose. "You

158

were an out-of-work actor who preferred to weave on your wife's looms than go out and look for jobs."

"That's because I wove better than I acted, only I had to marry you to find this out."

"Are you the only ones living on the old farm?"

Nelda Ross shook her head. "There are three other couples, a former professor of history at Columbia and his wife who's a pianist, a former advertising account executive and his wife and their two little boys, and the former owner of a big automobile agency in Westchester County and his wife and baby."

Budge looked at Dan skeptically. "You really like it up here in the backwoods better than you did down in New York?"

Dan leaned back in his chair, stretched one arm high over his head, and stroked his mustache lightly with the forefinger of his other hand. "I sure do."

"You don't make much money farming."

"We're not in it for the money."

"But you can't live without money."

"Oh, we have money," Louis said. "Heaps of money from the worldwide sale of the beautiful handwoven fabrics of Phyllis and Louis."

"Worldwide?" Budge looked incredulous.

"One order from Hawaii last week and another just today from Denmark."

Phyllis pushed him back in the chair. "He's a dreamer. But we do have all the orders we can fill."

"But why do you do it? I just don't understand. I can see coming up to the country for a vacation or even for a year or two off from business, but to bury

yourselves up here for the rest of your lives?" Budge shook his head wonderingly.

Louis leaned forward again. "It is, I think, like believing in religion. It is not a thing you can explain, n'est-ce pas? To the man who has faith, religion makes much sense, but to the man who has not faith, it is all foolishness. To you foolishness, to us truth."

"Suppose you change your minds after a few years and decide you don't like this life. Then what will you do? You'll have lost all your resources, all your contacts. You'll have to start all over again from the bottom."

"I guess it's a question of what's important to you," Dan said. "To us it was important to do this."

"But the same things are important to everyone. Or they should be. Every man wants a good job so he can provide well for his family and live comfortably and be respected by his neighbors. You can't argue with that."

"No, I can't." Thoughtfully, Dan caressed his beard between his thumb and forefinger. "But I do argue with the point of view that says there is only one right way to provide well for my family, live comfortably, and be respected by my neighbors. There are as many ways of doing a thing as there are people, you know, and who am I to say that one man's way is better than another's?"

"And think how dull it would be if we all did everything the same way." Nelda Ross got up from the floor where she had been sitting cross-legged and

161

brushed some pieces of bark and sawdust off her long wool skirt.

Dan looked at his watch and stood up, too. "Milking time, Louis. Don't forget it's your turn this afternoon."

Louis sighed. "Ah, oui, les petites vaches. Tout le temps, in need of milking."

"I suppose you'd like to live the way those people are living," Budge said when they had gone.

"I don't know as I'd make a very good farmer." Marc brushed the dirt off the last two potatoes and put them in a pan of water to boil.

"But would you be happy living like that?"

"I don't know, Dad. I'd have to try it before I could say."

"But how do you want to live? What will make you happy?"

"I don't know. I haven't had enough experience to be able to say."

"Then how can you say you wouldn't be happy at home if you came back?"

"I would be happy if you and Mom would just leave me alone to do things my own way. It's not as if I broke any laws with my hair and my clothes and my ideas."

"We only did it to make things easier for you, to save you from making a fool of yourself in the eyes of the world."

"Dad, the people I care about don't make that kind of judgment."

162

"Nonsense. Everyone makes judgments."

"Not everybody makes the kind of personal judgments you're talking about."

"Listen, buddy, I've been around a lot longer than you have, and I've seen a lot more people and I know there isn't anybody who doesn't make personal judgments."

Marc threw himself into the armchair. "Dad, how can I come home if you go on talking like that?"

"What's wrong?" Budge shut his mouth with a snap and bent down to pull the tackle box out from under his chair and set it on his knee. "All right, so I make strong statements occasionally. You don't have to take them so seriously."

"Yeah, I guess you're right."

Budge pawed through the gear in the box. "There are a couple of hooks here and plenty of line. We'll need an ax tomorrow to chop holes in the ice. Is there one around anywhere?"

"Maybe there's one in the boathouse. How many slices of bacon do you want for supper?"

"Four or five." Budge looked up. "Say, aren't you ever going to take off that hat?"

Marc flushed. "You know why I've got it on."

Budge slammed shut the lid of the tackle box. "I suppose you're always going to hold that incident against me?"

"No, I don't hold anything against you, but I'm not going to give you a chance to do something like that to me again."

"Now listen here. If you expect to live under my roof and enjoy the advantages of being my son, you're going to have to do what I say."

"Dad, I'm your son but I'm not your personal possession."

"You're my son," Budge said stubbornly.

"I'm also Marc Ainsworth."

"What's the difference?"

"You really don't see any?"

"I suppose I do," Budge growled. "Now, are you going to take off that hat?"

"When I go to bed. It's keeping my ears warm."

Budge jumped up, his hand raised and his fingers outstretched to snatch the hat off Marc's head. Marc lifted his chin and stared at his father without moving. Budge's hand dropped and he turned away.

Marc finished cutting the bacon and threw the strips into the frying pan. Budge wandered around the room, then stood at the window drumming on the glass with his fingers.

"Okay," he said without turning around. "Maybe I have been too bossy. After all, you are nearly grown-up and I suppose sometime I've got to learn to shut up and let you learn by experience what the right way to do things is. Now will you change your mind and come home?"

Marc poked at the strips of bacon with a fork. "Can I wait until we see what kind of luck we have tomorrow with the ice fishing?"

"Why, I guess that could be arranged." Budge

turned around and they grinned at each other through the cloud of blue smoke rising out of the sizzling frying pan.